SUBPOENAED WITH MY STEPBROTHER

SUBMITTING TO MY STEPBROTHER

BOOK FOUR

M. FRANCIS HASTINGS

To all my single ladies who could use a Caleb.

CONTENTS

A PUDDLE OF SOMETHING

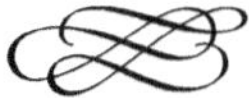

-Jacey-

I froze, and so did Caleb, the smiles wiped right off our faces.

Mike and Ed noted the change and quickly drew their weapons. "What's wrong?" Ed asked, his voice clipped.

"The only people who say that to us are the bad guys," I gulped. "The puddle of puppies thing."

All congeniality left the room as Bea went for her weapon, but the other woman drew down on her first. "I suppose I should start watching my language from now on," she smirked.

"Please don't be the Trinary. Please don't be the Trinary," I prayed aloud.

"What? No, nothing like that. Mr. Masterson just wants you both to come home," the woman said.

Bea walked forward so the woman's gun was right against her forehead. "Men, after she kills me, I want you to mow down every one of these bastards and get the kids out of here."

"No!" I cried.

Caleb moved so he was blocking me with his body.

I didn't see the men coming up behind the three new 'handlers' from the woods. I did see them when they got inside the house and pointed their semi-automatic weapons at the newcomers.

"You don't really want to be arrested, do you?" Bea asked as the woman turned to see what we were all looking at.

While she was distracted, Bea grabbed the gun and wrenched it away from her, turning it on the woman who'd been holding it on her.

The woman curled her lip. "Nice. Earpiece?"

"Every waking moment. I'm thinking of having it surgically implanted," Bea replied.

"Of course you know, we're not about to get caught," the woman said.

"Of course," Bea agreed.

The new male handlers went for their guns.

Guns went off all around us, and then, in a spray of blood, the alleged new handlers were dead.

Bea, who had blown a hole right through the woman's head, tucked the woman's gun into the waistband of her skirt. "We need to leave," she said urgently.

Caleb and I just stared at the carnage.

"*Now!*" she ordered.

"Right." Caleb lifted me up in his arms and picked his way through the viscera as quickly as he could, following Bea out of the cabin.

The perimeter guards formed a circle around us with Mike and Ed inside it with Caleb and me, Bea taking point. She led us quickly into the woods.

A loud explosion rocked the terrain just as we got inside the tree line, and I looked over Caleb's shoulder to see the cabin blown sky high.

"Was that us or them?" Caleb asked.

"Could be either. In any case, they've done us a favor. Now, move!" Bea said.

"I can walk, Caleb," I reminded him.

"Yep, you sure can," he agreed without putting me down.

I felt the tickle of air against my toes as Caleb jogged with me in his arms and came to the realization that he was wearing slippers, but I was barefoot.

At least Caleb was still keeping his head in all the confusion.

Bea led us to a nondescript, grassed-over back road, at the side of which was a blanket of rough camouflage. She yanked the blanket away to reveal two SUVs.

"Please don't separate us again," Caleb asked, still miles ahead of the situation. I was still seeing the new handlers dead on the floor of the cabin.

"No choice. We'll reconvene at the next safe house," Bea said. "We need at least one of you to bear witness against Masterson, and that means we can't keep you together right now."

Caleb's grip on me tightened, but I rubbed his back soothingly. "It's okay. We'll be back together at the next location, like she said."

He looked at me, and I knew there was something he wasn't saying. He was worried about something more than just us getting separated.

"It's going to be fine," I tried to reassure him.

"You can't promise that. No one can," Caleb murmured. But he finally loosened his grip. "We're wasting time here. I'll go with Mike and Ed. You take Jacey."

"Giving orders now?" Bea raised an eyebrow.

"Yeah. Yeah, I am," he replied.

"Fine. Get her in that SUV. Mike, Ed, if I don't see you at the next safe house, I'm going to be very pissed off, you understand? *Very* pissed off." She opened the back door behind the passenger seat, and Caleb gingerly placed me inside.

He then fused his lips to mine, his hand at the nape of my neck to anchor me in place. "You make it in one piece. And you give that bastard what for in court, with or without me," he whispered, his breath feathering my skin. Then he buckled me in, and with a sad expression, closed the door.

"Caleb?" I asked, wondering what was bothering him. I wished he would tell me.

But he either didn't hear me or didn't want to answer because he went over to the other SUV without a word and got himself in the back passenger side.

Bea slid behind the wheel of our SUV, and the engine soon roared to life.

"What isn't Caleb telling me?" I asked as she pulled onto the hidden road, slowly following it through the woods.

"Caleb is a very bright young man," she responded, eyes scanning the trail ahead as low-hanging branches and shrubs scraped against the side of the SUV. "He thinks the mole might be one of the three of us."

The blood left my face, and my heart pounded. "You mean he thinks the mole is either Mike or Ed."

"I knew I liked you. No surprise over there being a mole at all," Bea said.

"I've been around the block a few times." I curled my fingernails into my thighs, hoping the pain would mitigate the panic I felt in my chest. "Which one do you think it is?"

"Hard to say. I've worked with those men for years. We've been a team for nearly a decade." Her hands squeaked on the steering wheel as she gripped it harder. "I'd guess it was one of the perimeter guards, but Caleb wasn't willing to risk your pretty head on that possibility. He assumed the worst. Frankly, in his position, I'd have done the same."

Oh, Caleb. "He thinks he's going back to Masterson. And he didn't take me with him."

"That boy has it bad for you. He had that walk-through-fire expression on his face. I'm hoping neither of my men are the leak and that he'll arrive at our next destination as planned," Bea said.

"Are we going to the same destination?" I asked.

Her lip lifted a little on one side. "Smart girl. I'd have made different plans for the two of you to be separated, but Ed and Mike know where the next safe house is. If they don't arrive with Caleb, or there's some kind of ambush, then I'll know."

"So... you're trying to flush out the mole with me?" I replied.

"Yes. But don't worry. I'm not just going to drive up to the place with you." She crooked her head in my direction briefly. "I'm stashing you in a motel in the next town."

"You're... what?" I blinked at her.

"We both know this might be a hell of a showdown if one of my men is involved. So I'm keeping you out of the way of any whizzing bullets. If I'm lucky, the men will just arrive with Caleb as planned, and we can get both of you to a location not even my superiors know about. If things go bad... well... I'm going to leave you with a number to call if you don't hear from me within twenty-four hours," Bea said.

I dug my fingernails deeper into my thighs. I was not freaking out. I was not freaking out. Now was not the time to freak out. "How will I know the number goes to someone who isn't in on it?"

"Because if that person is in on it, there's no hope for the nation as a whole," she assured me.

"That's... both reassuring and frightening," I mumbled.

"Most things in this business are." The SUV thudded over a small fallen branch, causing the whole vehicle to rock, and Bea swore.

I grappled with the oh-shit bar, but the upset was over almost as soon as it had begun. "I hope the motel doesn't mind me coming in without luggage. I don't want to draw attention."

"The motel I'm taking you to would be more surprised if you did show up with luggage," she said.

"Oh. A by-the-hour place?" I asked, rubbing the back of my neck. I wasn't going to be at all comfortable in a place like that. I looked down at my modest clothes. I wouldn't fit in as a streetwalker.

"Not quite, but close. Anyway, you won't be leaving your room, so you'll have nothing to worry about," she replied.

I nodded. "I can do that."

We emerged through the trees and onto a grated dirt road, and Bea took a hard left, sending gravel flying.

I grasped the oh-shit bar again. "We in a hurry?"

"To get away from what's left of the cabin? Yes. I don't want any more Masterson goons popping out of the shadows. Best way to avoid that is to get ourselves on the highway," she explained.

I felt sorry for anyone following in our dust trail, because when I looked behind us, it looked as though we were creating a sandstorm. I didn't let go of the oh-shit bar, feeling the SUV fishtail ever so slightly over the dirt. Bea was keeping us at a pace that was almost dangerous, I could feel it, though her face in the rearview mirror showed nothing but control.

When we finally hit the highway, I was nearly faint with relief. Sure, she was still speeding, but now it felt like all four wheels were under us, which gave me a much better sense of wellbeing.

We exited the highway less than an hour later, and Bea circled behind a very sketchy-looking bar into the parking lot for the Waystop Motel. Or rather WAP MOL, from the missing letters. I looked at the two-level dingy building with outfacing doors to the rooms (rooms that had three deadbolts on the door), and decided that if I owned a place this run-down, I wouldn't have thought replacing the lights in the sign would help much, either.

"Stay here." Bea got out of the SUV and locked the doors then went to the main office.

Her being gone the less than ten minutes it took to get a key had me hyperventilating. When she returned and unlocked the SUV, holding a pair of flip-flops and a set of keys, I nearly leaped from the vehicle. Bea held me back and presented me with the flip-flops. "Wear these. Last thing we need is you slicing your foot open on a broken beer bottle."

"Oh. Right. Thanks." I slid the flip-flops on.

The keys jangling from Bea's fingers boldly stated "107" on the keychain. We walked to the room, and she jiggled two different keys in the locks to get the door to open.

When we got inside, she quickly pulled the drapes closed and gestured for me to sit on the bed, which had a comforter riddled with cigarette burns.

"If I don't come back in twenty-four hours, call this number," Bea said, pressing a business card into my hands. "Lock the door behind me, including setting the bar against the door. Don't open the door for anyone except me and the man on that card. You understand?"

I nodded, clutching the business card to my chest.

She squeezed my shoulder. "If all goes well, I'll be back in a couple of hours."

"Okay. And in twenty-four, I call this guy," I repeated.

"Good girl." Then Bea left.

Per her orders, I locked the door and put the bar under the knob just in case. Then, still not feeling quite safe enough, I started pushing furniture in front of the door as well, uncovering stains I didn't want to try to recognize.

"Caleb," I sighed, sitting cross-legged on the bed after I was finished. "Please be okay.

MOLE HUNTING

-Caleb-

"So," I said conversationally once Mike and Ed had us on the road, "which one of you is the mole?"

Mike turned back to look at me while Ed, who was driving, flicked a glance at me in the rearview mirror.

"Um... I think Jacey might have screwed your brains out, kid, because you're talking to two loyal agents." Mike frowned.

"You're probably right about that," I conceded. "But I still have enough cells to rub together to know somebody spilled the beans."

"It was probably one of the perimeter guards," Ed sighed. "Though it pains me to say it."

The possibility had occurred to me. But given everything Jacey and I had been through, the skeptic in me wasn't holding out much hope. "That would be a convenient explanation," I said.

Mike looked over at Ed. "I think the kid's lost his marbles."

"I think he's smarter than he looks," Ed replied, glancing at me in the rearview mirror again.

"Experience has taught me that if there is a way I can be screwed, I will be screwed. And I wasn't about to take Jacey down that path this time," I stated.

Mike sniggered. "Looking at that piece you've been keeping to yourself, I'm pretty sure you are getting screwed every which way to Sunday. I say again, you've lost your damn mind."

"Actually, he hasn't." Ed pulled a gun out of his shoulder holster and pointed it at Mike.

There it was. The moment I'd been dreading. I couldn't say I liked Mike much, but that didn't mean I was looking forward to seeing his brains painted against the passenger window.

The poor asshole didn't even get out a full squawk of surprise before he was little more than hamburger on a torso.

"Clean that up. We don't want to draw attention on the highway," Ed said flatly, not one spark of remorse in his tone.

"Yessir." It was going to be one of those days. I looked around for something to wipe up Mike with, then settled on my own shirt. I pulled it over my head and started cleaning the window.

"Masterson said you were both brighter than you looked. And he was right. How did you know it wasn't Bea?" Ed asked.

I finished cleaning the window and sat back again, dropping my shirt on the floor and toeing it over behind the driver's seat. "Bea walked right up to a gun and stuck her forehead between us and danger. I figured of the three of you, she was the least likely. Though I really had been hoping it was Mike. Or one of the perimeter guards. Or Mike."

He grunted. "Glad I didn't have to shoot Bea. Mike's an ass, but we've been working together for nearly a decade now. Can't say as I enjoyed that. I won't enjoy blowing your brains out, either, if you make that necessary."

"How much is he paying you?" I asked.

"None of your business. I will tell you it's a lot sweeter if I have both of you. And I will have both of you," he said.

"Good luck with that. Bea's probably taking Jacey all the way to FBI headquarters after this. I think it's just going to be you and me." I smirked, feeling superior. I'd at least taken Jacey out of the game. Finally.

I needed her to be safe.

"Bea is going to take her to the safe house. She has a policies and procedures stick so far up her ass that it's coming out the top of her head," he snorted.

I shook my head. "Wanna bet on that? Bea's not taking Jacey anywhere near that safe house."

"You'll lose," Ed said.

"Well, then it's a safe bet for you. I tell you what. If Jacey's there, I'll convince her to come with us quietly. But if she's not, you let me go and fuck off somewhere Masterson can't find you. Because I imagine he'll be pretty disappointed if you lost me," I responded.

He gave me a hard look in the rearview mirror. "You really don't think Bea's going to take her there?"

"I swear on my sex life." I folded my arms defiantly across my chest.

That made him snort. "I suppose I should be wary then. Bea may not trust me."

"You think rolling up without Mike is going to help matters?" I scoffed.

"Hmm. You have a point there." But Ed merely shrugged. "I'll deal with Bea. If she's not bringing Jacey, then she'll be alone. I like those odds."

"She might bring down the whole force on your head," I warned him.

He shook his head. "She'd want to be sure first. Oh, and speaking of being sure, much as I'd love for you to try to get us into an accident, I think I might like it better if you were restrained." He tossed a pair of cuffs into the back seat. "Cuff your wrists to the oh-shit bar."

"Or?" I asked.

"Or Masterson wasn't specific about how many pieces I could return you in." Ed growled.

I sighed and cuffed one wrist, threaded the other cuff over the oh-shit bar, and then snapped the other cuff onto my other wrist so my arms were dangling in the air. "Happy now?"

"Much better. You might want to get some sleep. Masterson's

probably not going to let you get much when you get to his place," he said.

There was wisdom in those words. Still, I only pretended to close my eyes and sleep, watching Ed through slitted lids. He wasn't going to get the drop on me anytime soon.

We stopped in front of a dilapidated old house with an overgrown yard and a listing chain link fence. He turned off the motor and peered at the house, which was completely dark.

"Think we beat them here?" I asked.

"I knew you weren't sleeping. Your loss, kid." He kept eyeballing the house. "The way Bea drives? Unlikely we're the first people here."

"You could uncuff me, and I could go find out for you," I suggested sweetly.

Ed rolled his eyes at me. "Nice try, kid." He stepped out of the SUV.

As he walked down the path to the house, I started wrenching at the oh-shit bar, trying to get away. Unfortunately, either the SUV was made with really strong oh-shit bars, or the FBI fortified them with something because the stupid thing wouldn't budge.

I was so focused on the task at hand that I didn't notice anyone else around the SUV until the driver's door opened. My head snapped around, and I saw Bea.

"He killed Mike…" I began, but she put a finger to her lips. She fished in her pocket, then came up with a handcuff key.

Bea quickly uncuffed me then had me wriggle to the front to follow her out the driver's door, I supposed to keep the sound of another door opening from Ed. I glanced at Mike's remains as I passed. "I'm so sorry," I whispered.

"Not your fault. Now let's get gone." She grabbed my wrist, and we slinked across the street to a beat-up old Corolla.

"Get in the back. Head down," she said. Bea quickly hopped in the front, and, just as Ed was coming back out of the house, a look of confusion on his face, she floored it.

The Corolla fishtailed around in a half circle. I ducked while Bea aimed over my head to shoot out Ed's tires.

Ed dove to the ground before she could shoot him, but she was more focused on getting us out of there than getting into a gunfight with him.

I had to give her credit for that. If it had been me, I'd have stayed to shoot the bastard full of holes for what he did to Mike.

Then again, as the back window shattered, I remembered Ed also had a gun, and perhaps, discretion was the better part of valor.

"Don't worry. He'll get his. Keep your head down," Bea said as though she'd read my mind.

I pressed my face to the upholstery. "Is Jacey okay?"

"She's fine. I thought it best not to get her caught in the middle of this mess," she replied.

"Good thinking." I still felt bad about Mike.

"Ed's not going to take the SUV anywhere. I'll call for a pick up. Mike will be properly buried," Bea said.

"You really are psychic, you know that?" I murmured.

She gave a sad chuckle. "You're not the first person to think so."

I figured the first person was probably Mike, judging from her tone, so I decided not to press the issue.

The trip wasn't long. Within ten minutes, Bea and I were standing in front of a shit pile of a motel.

"She's here?" I asked.

"She's here," Bea confirmed. "And you two are staying here until I can get another team to come get you. One led by a guy I trust."

"Sounds like a plan." I followed her to Room 107.

Bea knocked on the door. "Jacey? It's me."

The curtains twitched, and I saw just a glimpse of a very intact Jacey. A tightness I didn't even know I was holding left my chest.

"Just a sec!" Jacey called through the door. "I... uh... sorta rearranged the furniture."

Bea chuckled. "You're both smart kids."

"Experience is a great teacher," I remarked.

After a few minutes, the bolts on the door finally snapped open, and Jacey opened the door. Her eyes went straight to me, and she, too, relaxed.

"Caleb." Jacey's lower lip quivered.

I stepped forward and opened my arms but got a hard smack across the cheek instead. "Ow."

"How *dare* you put yourself in danger like that!" Jacey shouted as I rubbed my cheek. "You could have been killed!"

"I think you two need to take this inside," Bea said, waving Jacey away from the door so we could both step in. "I can see you're going to head into one hell of a fight, so I'll just take my leave now. You'll be hearing from me."

"Thanks, Bea," I replied, my cheek still smarting.

Bea looked at the red-faced Jacey, the wincing me, and shook her head. "Good luck," she said to me before stepping back out.

I closed the door and bolted all the locks, even the bar that went under the doorknob. "I can explain…"

Once I turned around, Jacey launched herself at me, pounding my chest with her fists. "Explain?! You went with the enemy! On purpose!!!"

I grabbed her wrists to stop her from hitting me. "Jacey, love, it was either you or me."

"You didn't tell me! You made the decision without me!" she snapped, tears rolling down her cheeks. "How could you do that?"

"There wasn't a lot of time to discuss it," I reminded her. I wrapped my arms around her, pinning her fists between us, and cradled her head against my shoulder. "I love you. I didn't want anything to happen to you."

"You don't think I feel the same way?!" she argued, her tears sliding down my bare skin.

"I know you do." I nuzzled her hair gently. "Forgive me? I would have convinced you if we'd had time."

Jacey pouted up at me, a stubborn set to her jaw. "No, you wouldn't have."

"Hmm. Maybe not. But it's over now. Do you really want to argue about it?" I asked, giving her my best puppy-dog expression. "Or would you rather kiss and… make up?"

She pursed her lips, anger still flashing behind her tears. Then she sighed and lifted her lips to mine.

NEED

-Jacey-

I considered telling Caleb if he ever did anything stupid like that again, he was never getting any for the rest of his life. But that would have been a blatant lie, and we'd have both known it. As our kiss transitioned from forgiveness to want to need his hand smoothed down my back and cupped my ass, pulling my hips tight to his so I could feel his hardening length against my stomach.

"I knew you just wanted to have hero sex," I grumbled, rubbing my hands over his chest and nipples.

He chuckled, his pupils dilating with a need I could feel all the way in my core. "What's 'hero sex'?"

"You know. When the hero does some big feat of... heroics... and then climbs up the tower, grabs the damsel..." I began to explain as Caleb divested me of my shirt.

"Mhm. And then what does the hero do after he grabs the damsel?" he asked.

"Hero... stuff." I gasped, arching my back as he pushed up my bra to palm my bare breasts.

"Does he kiss her?" he teased, pressing his lips to mine as he backed me to the bed.

I nodded. "Mhm."

"What else does he do?" Caleb kissed his way down to nibble at the curve of my shoulder and neck.

"Um... he..." I panted. "Pretty sure he... gets to... ravish her."

"Lucky hero." He leaned me down until my back was flat on the comforter. Then he started sucking my nipples.

I gasped and spiked my fingers into his hair, holding him to me. Caleb tugged my pants and panties down far enough for me to wriggle them off. Then I heard his zipper.

"Just... to clarify. I'm still mad at you," I muttered as he lifted one of my knees over his hip.

"I know. But you're just as cute when you're angry," he beamed. He pressed the head of his thick cock against my entrance, and suddenly, I could barely remember my own name, much less why I was angry with him.

"Caleb," I whined, bucking my hips a little to take him in.

The man would not be rushed. He cradled my hips in his hands, effectively stopping me from claiming him with my pelvis, and began easing into me at a torturous pace.

"You know," I protested. "I'm going to be angry with you for a TOTALLY DIFFERENT reason if you don't get your big dick up in me RIGHT THIS SECOND!"

He laughed. "Is my baby hungry?"

"Yes!"

"I can feel you trying to suck me in. Such a good girl. You deserve a reward, don't you?" he teased.

I gripped Caleb's wrists. "Yes. Reward me, damn it!"

"Language." But I didn't care what he thought. He gave me my treat, and that was all I cared about.

His cock stretched me as though my core had forgotten how big he was–despite the fact we'd made love not twenty-four hours ago.

"Always so tight," he groaned, forcing himself as deep as he could go with his grip on my hips.

I loved it. I needed it. I wrapped my legs around his waist and begged him to ride me. Hard.

Caleb, ever obliging, started ramming me with his big cock. His balls slapped against me as he found a punishing pace that we both enjoyed.

"Give it to me," I encouraged him when I felt myself nearing the edge. "Caleb, oh God." I came hard, my whole body shaking and shivering.

He wasn't far behind me. I was still trembling when he cried out and I felt his hot seed jet into me.

I breathed hard, running a shaking hand over the sweaty tendrils of hair that had escaped onto my forehead.

Caleb didn't pull out. I hardly expected him to. Not after just one round.

"I don't suppose you want to see if the TV is w—" I began.

"Fuck the TV."

I shrieked as Caleb lifted me off the bed and into his arms, my legs locked around his waist keeping him inside me as he executed the maneuver.

It was then that I knew something wasn't quite right. He was still stiff inside me, but his expression was haunted.

"Caleb?" I asked, frowning slightly. "What's wrong?"

"Ed killed Mike," he replied flatly.

"Oh." I didn't know what to say to that.

"In front of me."

My eyes widened. "Oh my God."

Caleb swallowed as he walked us into the tiny bathroom and into the tinier shower. "He made me clean it up."

My heart constricted, and I hugged him tightly. "I'm sorry. I'm so sorry. Oh God."

"I just need to forget for a while, Jacey. Is that okay?" he whispered, kissing me and moving his thumb in to rub my clit. "Just for a little while."

"You can 'forget' until they come to get us," I assured him. I kissed Caleb fiercely.

"What if it takes weeks?" he asked with a hitch of sad laughter.

"Then I'll be sore and tired but happy," I said.

He gave a bark of real laughter then and turned on the shower.

We both flinched at the cold water. But, of course, we expected it to warm up.

In a minute.

Or two.

Or… seven?

We looked at each other, and Caleb shook his head just as the water pressure decreased to a trickle of lukewarm discomfort.

"I guess this is what we get," he said.

I cupped my hands and got enough water to wet his hair. I massaged it into his scalp, and he groaned and pushed me back against the wall, sinking deeper inside me.

"It's just you and me," I told him. "All the ugliness is outside. Here, it's just you and me."

The cool tile at my back was a stark contrast to the heat of Caleb against and inside me. "Baby, don't stop. That feels so good." His hips moved, and my eyelids fluttered, his cock rubbing against the very spot I wanted it to with every thrust.

I kept massaging his scalp, kissing him and rubbing my breasts against his slippery skin.

"You always know just what I need." He groaned, biting my shoulder as he came hard inside me.

My own orgasm wasn't far behind, and we held each other under the trickle of warm water. Until it went cold again, of course.

Caleb laughed and shook water out of his hair like a dog. "Much as I like what this cold water's doing to your nipples, I'd rather my baby not get sick." He pulled out gently then set me on the floor slowly, rubbing my body against every inch of his.

Every inch of his still wanted me, and as he turned off the water, I rubbed his shaft. "I can make you feel good," I promised.

"You always make me feel good. Even when we're not having sex." He smiled back at me and grabbed a scratchy towel off the metal rack above the toilet. He did his best to wrap me in it, but it was small to begin with and seemed to have shrunk with multiple washings. I knew it was meant to be a white towel, but it had gone grayish.

"I don't suppose they have some big, soft, Hilton-grade terry cloth robes in this place," he muttered, grabbing a towel for himself while I tried, unsuccessfully, to keep my boobs from popping out of mine.

"Pretty sure we're out of luck on that one," I replied. I took my hand away from his cock so he could wrap his towel around his waist. But, eyes twinkling with mischief, Caleb took my hand and inserted it between the folds of the towel so I could wrap my hand around his thick dick again.

"I never said I wanted you to stop." He grinned and stared down at my bare breasts.

My nipples hardened under his gaze, and my cheeks flushed. He still wanted me. I still wanted him. And we had hours, perhaps even days, before anyone came for us.

"You don't want to watch TV?" I breathed, teasing my fingers over his hard cock.

"We won't be needing that." His breath hitched, and I could tell he was close.

"What if we're here for weeks?" I asked with wide-eyed innocence. I slowly dropped to my knees.

"Then they'll need to replace every piece of furniture in this room." Caleb sucked in a deep breath as I took him in my mouth. "Oh, baby, your mouth feels like heaven."

I suppressed a grin as he tangled his fingers in my hair, fucking my mouth and throat while I squeezed his balls and did my best to pleasure him with my lips and tongue. It still made me feel so powerful that performing this small act could reduce my love to a puddle of pudding.

It didn't take long before he released his salty, hot seed down my throat. He threw his head back and shouted as I swallowed, missing only a few drops that dribbled out the side of my mouth.

Caleb caught them on his thumb, and I licked them away. "I am a lucky sonofabitch," he whispered and pulled me up to kiss him.

BACK TO MINNESOTA

-Caleb-

The door banged, shaking on its hinges despite the three deadbolts and the bar fortifying it.

I blinked awake at the same time Jacey did, both of us sitting up, naked. "Get in the bathroom," I said urgently to her. "I'll handle this."

"What? Caleb, we don't know who's out there!" she hissed back at me. But I gave her a shove in the direction of the bathroom just the same, and she tumbled off that way, cursing under her breath. "If you get killed, Caleb Killeen, I will never forgive you!"

"Love you, too," I called after her. "Lock the door behind you."

It was only after I heard the lock turn that I padded over to the door and peered through the peephole.

There was an entire SWAT team waiting outside the door behind Bea and an older, well-dressed man who was likely in his sixties. Both of their outfits screamed FBI.

"Hi Bea," I said through the door. "Just give us a minute, okay? We need to shower and get dressed."

"No time. We're attracting too much attention. Throw on what you've got, and let's go," Bea replied.

I sighed. I'd been afraid she'd say that. "Jacey? Get dressed. We've gotta go!"

"But… shower!" she protested.

"Bea says no," I replied.

"Aww." Jacey came out of the bathroom and started gathering up her clothes with an unhappy pout.

I traced my fingers down her naked back. "I'm sure they're going to let us shower at the next location."

"Oh, I know just what you want to do at the next location, Caleb Killeen, and don't you think for one second we're doing anything before I get a nice, hot shower," she said primly, pulling on her panties.

"We'll shower together and call it even," I amended and she rolled her eyes at my grin.

"Fine," she agreed.

I mean, it wasn't as though either of us had harbored any doubts about it.

"Aren't you going to get dressed?" she asked.

I'd been so engrossed in watching Jacey's tits jiggle as she wrangled them into her bra that I hadn't touched my own clothing. I was also now sporting a semi.

"Oh no you don't," Jacey said, her eyes zeroing in between my legs. "If there isn't time for a shower, then there's definitely no time for that." She tossed my boxers at me. "Suck it up, buttercup."

"Sassy." I smiled at her and started pulling on my own clothes.

A fist banged on the door again. "Are you two ready yet?!" Bea called.

"Just about!" I zipped my jeans and helped Jacey hook her bra behind her back after she got frustrated. Then I handed Jacey her shirt. "Okay, shoes and let's go."

"I still just have the flip-flops," she grumbled, slipping on a neon green pair.

"They'll get you something better," I assured her. I pulled on my tennis shoes, then undid the locks, moved the bar, and opened the door.

The older gentleman looked Jacey and me up and down, his lips pursed. "Well, at least you're both still in one piece." He poked his head in the room, looking past my shoulder. "I'm not seeing any condoms. Do we need to make arrangements for prenatal care?"

"Excuse me?" I gaped.

"We don't have time to pussyfoot around. Just answer the question," the older gentleman said.

"Not right now," I said at the same time Jacey shrugged and said, "Mirena."

"Mirena is an IUD. It's a birth control that lasts five years. Jacey shouldn't be getting pregnant any time soon," Bea clarified.

"Good. It's harder to move you around with a kid on the way." The older gentleman stuck out his hand. "Hansen."

"Caleb," I introduced myself, shaking his hand.

Jacey shook hands next. "Jacey," she said.

"Good. Now we're all acquainted. Let's get out of here." Hansen made a circle-up motion to the SWAT team and we walked through the parking lot to a series of black SUVs.

"Do we have to go in separate cars again?" Jacey asked, sounding about as happy at the prospect as I felt.

"No. That's what the team is for. We're driving you to the airport. You'll be met by another group in Minneapolis," Hansen said. "Or, rather, we will. Bea and I will be your handlers from now on."

"Do we know when and where Masterson's trial is happening yet?" I asked.

"Different districts are fighting for the privilege, but doubtless this shit is going to make it all the way to the Supreme Court. You'll probably be testifying several times, both of you," Hansen said. "And, likely, we'll have to move you around a lot. But so far, it looks as though they're kicking things off in Minnesota, so we need you close by to give testimony when the time comes." He held open the back door of an SUV for Jacey and me.

I made sure Jacey was sitting behind the passenger seat—the safest place in the vehicle—and then took my place behind the driver's seat.

"I really do admire your courage," Hansen said as he got in the driver's seat. "A lot of people would have given up by now and refused to testify."

"That asshole is going to get his if I have to keep telling the world about his crimes until the day I keel over from Alzheimer's," I gritted out.

Jacey put a hand on my knee while Bea got in the passenger seat.

The rest of the posse loaded up in the other SUVs. The convoy ultimately consisted of five black SUVs, with ours being the middle one.

"Good for you," Hansen said, picking up the conversation again as soon as we were out on the highway. "I like that attitude."

Jacey leaned her cheek against my shoulder. I could tell she was tired.

"Get some sleep," I murmured. "I've got this."

She nodded and closed her eyes, her breath evening out in mere minutes.

"I don't think Jacey and I can have what we want to have without testifying against Masterson," I confessed once she was asleep. "I certainly don't want us living as his prisoners. He already made Jacey have a baby through invitro with his son." I thought of Will and it was as though someone ripped a Band-Aid off a hole in my chest. I rubbed the spot with a frown.

"High body count on all sides over this," Bea said sympathetically.

"Will was a good guy. No matter what his dad made him do, he was a good guy. I want to make sure the world knows that, too." My voice was soft, and, I realized, choked with unshed tears.

"I don't honestly know if he'll come up in court at all, but if he does, you can tell them what a good man Will was," Bea replied.

I rubbed tears from my eyes, tamping down on the horror and loss. There would be plenty of time to fall apart later. I needed to keep it together until this whole mess was over. "And, if possible, we'd like the baby."

"Will and Jacey's baby?" Hansen asked, craning his neck a bit to look at me.

"Yes. I don't want him growing up under that asshole's influence," I growled.

"Well, as long as a DNA test shows Jacey is the mother, once Masterson has been put in prison—which is the hope, not a guarantee—then there should be little trouble getting Will Jr. into your custody," he said.

"Good." I took a deep breath. "And we need to get Hank, my mom, and our brother out of Masterson's compound. He's already hurt Hank badly enough to cripple him. I don't know what's going on with them right now, but I can only hope since Masterson can't lord it over us, he's not torturing our family right now."

"Long list of demands you've got there," Hansen snorted.

I would have shrugged, and almost did, but remembered Jacey was sleeping on me at the last second. I brushed a kiss over her hair, dragging in the sweet scent that was entirely her. "I just want everyone to be okay when this is all over. I want the trafficking to stop, but I also don't want my mom living in fear every day of her life. If that makes sense."

"Makes sense to me," Bea said.

"We'll do what we can, of course," Hansen added. "But, like I said, there are no guarantees. Hell, I'm even afraid to guarantee your safety at this point after all the shit that's gone down. But I can tell you we'll do our best. And that's pretty fucking good most of the time."

I nodded slightly. "Thanks."

Bea and Hansen nodded back, then the SUV descended into silence as Hansen and the convoy took us to the airport.

We drove right onto the tarmac to a waiting jet. I gave Jacey a little jostle when the SUV stopped, and she woke up and rubbed her eyes. "Are we home?" she asked.

"Not quite," I said. "But we're getting on the plane that's taking us there. Wherever home's going to be for the next... well, I'd expect at least a few days. Maybe we'll be moving around a lot, but I think we can't hope for better than being in Bea's and Hansen's care."

Jacey nodded and followed me out of the vehicle, sliding across to the driver's side behind me. I took her hand, and with a platoon of armed guards surrounding us, and Bea and Hansen by our sides, we boarded the plane.

"Next stop, Minneapolis," Hansen stated once he got us all buckled in and settled.

"Home," Jacey breathed, and looked at me.

I nodded, acknowledging her unspoken terror. Going back to the place where it all began didn't exactly feel safe.

But we had to do it, or the madness that had become our life was never going to end.

MUSICAL SAFEHOUSES

-Jacey-

I didn't know they still had pay phones lurking around Minnesota, but, much to my surprise, Hansen stopped the new convoy from the airport to make a quick call at a gas station on one.

"I thought maybe you'd do a burner phone spy thing?" I said to Bea as Hansen was checking in.

"This is better," she informed me. "A burner phone can still be traced, and if we use it while we're around you, then they can triangulate our location. This way, Hansen just drives minutes or hours away to a random payphone, and no one knows where we're keeping you."

"So, he's checking in with your superiors?" Caleb asked.

Bea's lips quirked up into a smirk. "Fortunately, there are very few people who are 'superior' to Hansen. But yes, the uppity ups need an update every once in a while. At least to know you're alive. And it's also their opportunity to update us on trial dates and such."

"Sounds very efficient," Caleb said.

"I hope that's not sarcasm. I know it's not exactly as immediate as a cell phone would be, but it's safe. For the most part," Bea responded.

"I wasn't being sarcastic," Caleb defended himself.

Hansen returned to the SUV then and groaned as he slid into the driver's seat. "I'm getting too old for field work."

"Oh, you know you love it," Bea grinned.

Hansen grunted, but there was a tiny smile playing on his lips.

"I suppose the desk job must get pretty boring after a while," Caleb said.

Hansen arched an eyebrow in the rearview mirror. "About as boring as working for Masterson, I suppose. Except I get to bust the bastards who traffic in human beings rather than just listen to them mow down a shipment of them over the phone."

Caleb paled, and I squeezed his hand as we left the gas station and got on the road once more.

"Is that what really happened?" I whispered when he didn't comment on the subject. He'd completely clammed up.

"Yes." But that was all he would say.

"Oh, love." I unbuckled my seatbelt and crawled into his lap, wrapping my arms around him.

Caleb frowned, though his eyes were still haunted. "Jacey, this isn't safe. You should sit back down and buckle up."

"Like we're ever safe," I scoffed and just hugged him tighter.

He sighed and buried his face in my chest.

"I love you." I kissed him on top of his head. "You're a good man, Caleb."

"Not so sure about that, but I'm trying to be," came his muffled voice from my cleavage.

"See this," Hansen said quietly, perhaps thinking we couldn't hear while we were in our own little world, "is why this is going to work. There's two of them supporting each other."

"I completely agree," Bea replied. "It won't be like last time."

Caleb and I both looked up. "Last time?"

Hansen and Bea looked at each other. Then Hansen gave Bea the slightest of nods.

She turned to us. "We had a witness against the sheik two years ago. He… killed himself after a year. He just couldn't handle it."

My throat went dry, but Caleb wrapped his arms around my

waist and held me tightly. "Nobody's killing themselves. Those bastards are going to trial, then jail, then hell, in that order," he declared.

"Right now, we can only focus on Masterson. We don't have jurisdiction over the sheik, though, no doubt, you will be called upon to be witnesses against him as well. The CIA is salivating over you. But we get you first," Hansen said.

"I feel like steak," I muttered.

"Ditto," Caleb agreed.

"I know it's not ideal, but it's the way things are for now, unfortunately," Bea informed us.

I hugged Caleb tightly and both of us remained silent for the rest of the trip.

The convoy left us at a hotel in the heart of Minneapolis. I felt as though I was the president arriving with all the fanfare that went along with getting us into the hotel. FBI agents, complete with earpieces and suits, surrounded us as soon as Hansen opened the car door for us. Eerily absent, however, were press or paparazzi trying to take our pictures. In fact, I noted a passerby raise his iPhone to take our picture, only to be mugged by the FBI.

Two agents removed their jackets and put them over our heads, shielding us from view. I concentrated on not tripping over sidewalk cracks, stairs, or carpeting. We went through a revolving door and into the lobby, as far as I could tell from the changes in the flooring, and then were hustled into an elevator.

"So… that was going to keep us safe? Parading us out like celebrities?" Caleb asked once Bea, Hansen, he, and I were in the elevator with just four other FBI agents surrounding us.

"We're only staying here a night. And it was a bit of pomp and circumstance the higher-ups wanted. They want Masterson to know you're back and still willing to testify," Hansen sighed.

"We have had people break in through windows to get at us before. I think you guys did it at least twice," Caleb pointed out.

"That's why we're going to the twenty-ninth floor," Bea said.

Sure enough, the doors opened on the twenty-ninth floor, and we went, en masse, to a suite where FBI agents were already holding the doors open.

Inside, more agents surrounded the perimeter of the suite, even though we were twenty-nine floors up.

Caleb started for a window, but one of the agents standing next to the windows held up his hand. "We've got snipers, kid, but likely, so do they," he said.

That stopped me from moving any closer to the windows. I grabbed Caleb's wrist and pulled him back by me.

"You might want to take that shower now," Hansen suggested. "I'm going to brief our team."

"I thought it was just going to be you and Bea?" I asked, looking around at all the suits.

"After today, for the most part, it will be. But, the higher-ups wanted to give one big show of force to put Masterson on the defensive while we finish building a case against him," Hansen sighed. "So, welcome to The Foshay Hotel, I guess."

"All right." Caleb put an arm around my shoulders. "Where's our bathroom?"

Hansen looked expectantly at the person who appeared to be the FBI agent in charge of our little show of force.

"That way," the agent said, pointing through a set of double doors. "That's your part of the suite. We ask that you don't leave it and keep the curtains drawn at all times. Do not look out the windows. This suite is specially equipped with bulletproof glass, but we don't need to tempt fate."

"Yessir," Caleb and I agreed together. Caleb steered me into the bedroom, past agents who looked as though they were still wanding the place for bugs, and into the large en suite bathroom with a large jacuzzi tub and a zero-entry multi-faucet shower.

Caleb stared down an agent who was checking the soaps until the man finally sighed and left the bathroom. Then, Caleb closed and locked the door.

I turned into his arms and leaned my forehead on his chest. "This is all getting so out of control."

"I know, baby. I know." He tilted my chin up to kiss me. "Let's just enjoy this place while we're here and try to go with the flow. We've got each other. Like Bea said, we're going to be okay."

"They make it sound like this is going to keep going on for years and years," I all but wailed. I hadn't meant to, really, but it was all getting ridiculous. "I mean, are we ever going to have our lives back?!"

He kissed me again, this time more deeply, anchoring me to him by a hand at the back of my neck. "I can't promise you anything more than they can," he whispered against my lips. "Except that I love you, and I will always love you. If we can be together these next few years, or however long it takes, that's what matters the most."

I melted into him, my body plastering itself to his as he said the words. Really, what did it matter as long as we were together? "I love you, too," I said, my eyes stinging. "Sorry, I was having a moment."

"You know I understand. And I'll probably have a few of those myself." Caleb nuzzled my neck. "Let's have a bath, all right, baby?"

I nodded and raised my arms so he could take my shirt off. Pressed to him as I was, I could feel his hardness even through his jeans.

The two days we'd gone without showering made me feel absolutely filthy, but he didn't seem to care. He backed me to the bathtub and leaned over until I was balancing on the edge, just so he could get the warm water going. He activated the waterfall feature, and, while the tub filled, we got a bit lost in kisses and caresses. By the time the tub was full enough to get in and turn the jets on, we were both naked and desperate.

He got into the tub and pulled me in after him, right down onto his cock. His warm, wet length filled me to the brim as I braced a knee on either side of his hips, gasping as he cupped my ass and pushed his hips up, filling me almost past capacity.

"Caleb," I whimpered. "It's too deep."

He raised a cheeky eyebrow at me and rolled his hips.

I threw back my head and groaned at the tingle of fireworks that elicited from the apex of my thighs.

"Shh," he murmured, a wet thumb circling my nipple as he kept tormenting my insides with his big dick. "You don't want the whole FBI team to know what we're doing, do you?"

Of course, he followed this up with another rocking motion of his hips and lightly biting my peaked nipple.

I slapped a hand over my mouth to muffle a moan.

"That's my girl." He kept fucking me slow and deep, and all I could do was bite my palm and grip his shoulder with my other hand. Caleb knew my body better than I did. He knew what I could take.

I was going to get him back later with some torment of my own, but after the FBI left. I didn't trust myself to keep quiet, and I doubted Caleb would have that capacity, either. Not once I was sucking on his balls.

"What are you thinking about?" he asked breathlessly.

I had the choice between answering him or keeping my teeth safely stuck in the palm of my hand. I decided to risk it. "I-I was thinking about-about sucking your balls," I gasped. "To-to get you back."

"Tease." He grinned at me, his eyes hooded with desire as he worked my body up and down his shaft.

"It's… only teasing… if you don't mean to do it," I said.

Caleb inclined his head thoughtfully. "That's true. I think we're both good at delivering on our promises." His thumb rubbed against my clit. "Don't you think?"

Taking my hand away had been a mistake. I gave a long, loud yowl of pleasure as I came around him.

A low bellow and the rush of his seed came from Caleb less than a second later. "Can't have the FBI thinking you don't satisfy your man," he panted after his cock gave one final twitch.

"Well, I'm pretty sure we've convinced them we both please each other just fine," I replied with a blush.

"Mhm." He absently ran his wet fingertip back and forth over my collarbone as we both came down. Then he said, "Now, I seem to remember you saying something about sucking my balls?"

HERE, THERE, AND EVERYWHERE

-Caleb-

Sleeping on the luxury bedding of The Foshay was like sleeping on a cloud. A cloud where I could cuddle with the woman I loved.

I watched Jacey dreaming happily on my chest in the early morning light that filtered through the curtains, not moving a muscle. I didn't want to disturb her. She deserved rest where she could get it. We both did.

Her long, black hair tickled over my abs, and I resisted the urge to comb my fingers through it. She was just so damn beautiful.

The moment was broken when Bea pushed a coffee trolley into our room. "Rise and shine."

Jacey stirred, and those brilliant green eyes looked up at me for a second, and, instantly, I wanted her. I just wanted to bury myself in all the love I saw there and cocoon it around me forever.

There were other places I wanted to bury myself, but Bea was there, and, apparently, we needed to be up and ready for the day. "We must be moving along soon," I said, pushing the heel of my hand down Jacey's back in a little morning massage.

Jacey arched like a cat into my touch, and I really, really wished

Bea wasn't there. Especially as Jacey's breasts rubbed against my chest.

"Yeah, no time for that. Get some coffee, get dressed, and let's go. They're packing us up breakfast as we speak," Bea replied.

"Roger that," I sighed.

Jacey rubbed her cheek against my shoulder then kissed my neck. The woman was not playing fair!

"I really mean it. No nookie until we get to the next location," Bea warned.

"Right, right." I tilted Jacey's chin up for a kiss, then let her go with a frustrated exhale.

She didn't seem to be any happier about the situation as she wriggled off me and started to get out from under the blankets.

"Um…J—" I began.

I shouldn't have bothered. She realized almost immediately that she was naked and Bea was still in the room.

We both looked expectantly at Bea. She held up a stern finger. "No nookie."

"No nookie," we repeated together.

Bea nodded and left the room.

Jacey looked down at the tent my dick had made of the bedding and gave a sigh. "Wasted opportunity."

"We'll have plenty more opportunities," I promised her. Reluctantly, we both got out of bed and started pulling on clothes, though I didn't think her struggle was quite as painful as mine as I forced my aroused self into boxers and a pair of jeans.

I poured coffee for both of us, even though Jacey made a face. "Coffee's not really my thing," she reminded me.

"We're both going to need the caffeine," I said but gave the concession of a large helping of cream and sugar in her coffee so that it was barely tan.

She sipped it and wrinkled her nose, but didn't stop.

I drank my coffee completely black.

"I don't know how you do that," she grumbled, setting her cup down several minutes after I'd downed my own coffee.

"Practice," I responded.

The door opened again, and Bea stuck her head in. "Are you ready?" she asked impatiently.

"Yes, we're ready," I said, taking Jacey's hand and threading my fingers through hers.

"Good. Let's go." Bea led us out of our room and back into the main suite where it looked like there was a different group of FBI agents, but it was hard to tell because they were all still mostly unsmiling men in suits.

Most of the group peeled off from their stations and surrounded us again. They hustled us down to the lobby where there were more FBI agents clearing the way of guests so we could go out the front door.

"Still doing the song and dance?" I asked Hansen.

"That we are," he grumbled back. "On the positive side of things, we won't be doing this again until the trial date, I hope."

"You intend to parade us out again for the trial? I thought the idea was for us not to get shot so we could testify," I said.

"Politics, kid. You might get it someday. Though, considering you want to be a doctor, maybe you won't be so involved in the politics of making government agencies look good to the taxpayers," he explained. "Besides, nobody's getting sho—"

Just as I'd feared, a shot rang out as soon as we walked out the doors of the Foshay Tower, striking the stone of the building with a loud crack.

Then my face was slammed into the pavement, FBI agents having tackled both Jacey and me to the ground.

Jacey turned her face to look at me, her eyes wide with fear. Her cheek was scratched and bleeding from the cement.

"It's okay, baby," I wheezed, the wind completely knocked out of me. I inched my hand out to grasp hers. "The FBI's going to take care of i—"

Our hands were wrenched apart when we were both dragged back to our feet. We were carried more than marched into a large, black

SUV by a swarm of FBI agents who all had their guns drawn. Including Bea and Hansen.

"Caleb?" Jacey asked uncertainly.

The glass on the passenger side back window of the SUV suddenly crackled, the glass spider-webbing from the impact of a bullet that had been stopped. I assumed the vehicle was armored or something, with bulletproof glass, because there were two more shots that just made chinks in the glass.

Still, I pushed Jacey to the floor and laid over the top of her, waiting for the madness to stop.

"Go, go, go!" Hansen snapped at Bea, who had worked her way into the driver's seat. He pulled on his seatbelt and glanced back at us. "As soon as the shots stop, I want you in your seats and buckled up, understand?"

"Yes, sir," I said.

It didn't take long to understand his concern. Jacey and I were both thrown back and forth between the seats on the floor of the SUV as Bea drove. I figured she must be doing some kind of evasive maneuvers, but my stomach was not as on board with her driving tactics as my brain was. I dizzily got off Jacey once I was sure we were safe, then got her into her seat behind Hansen and buckled her in.

We took a hard corner before I had the chance to buckle my own seatbelt. I clung to it like a rope off the edge of a cliff, swinging back and forth as Bea maneuvered through downtown Minneapolis, navigating the complicated maze of one-way streets like a racer at the Grand Prix.

Once we got out of downtown, I was finally able to buckle myself in properly. I leaned my head back against the backrest and panted.

Jacey touched my cheek. "You're bleeding," she said.

I grimaced. "So are you." I looked at Bea and Hansen. "So, was it worth all the pomp? Because I'm getting the feeling Masterson might have won that round. If the idea was to let us know not even the FBI can keep us safe."

"You're alive, aren't you?" Hansen grunted. Then he shook his head and swore. "I told them. I told them and I told them."

"Well, next time they'll probably listen," Bea said.

I ground my teeth and looked at my bleeding love. "If you're just going to wave us around in front of Masterson's snipers, I can tell you right now, I'm out. I'll take Jacey, and we'll take our chances. You all can go fuck yourselves."

"It won't happen again." Hansen scowled at the dashboard. "I'm going to make sure of that."

"Good. Then we have an understanding. You can tell your superiors to piss off," I said, taking Jacey's hand and holding it on the seat.

The car fell into a seething silence. Jacey broke it after a while. "Where are we going?"

"It's best we don't tell you," Bea replied. "The less you know, the better."

"We'll only be staying at the next location for three days at the most, anyway," Hansen said.

"And then another location?" Jacey asked.

Bea nodded. "And then another location."

"We're not setting down roots anywhere, are we," I said. It wasn't a question.

"Not until the trial is over. And even then, the CIA is asking for a piece of you after they've managed to nail the Sheik. So… I think I'd just start being ready to go at all times," Bea replied with a sympathetic wince in the rearview mirror.

"I know it's not ideal–" Hansen said.

"None of this is ideal," I interrupted him. "Damn Masterson anyway! If it weren't for him, I'd be in medical school right now, Jacey and I would be married, and we'd be in family housing at the university working on our two-and-a-half kids."

"That sounds nice," Jacey agreed. "When can we do that?"

Hansen looked back at us. "You're both still very young. You've got plenty of time. Just consider this as a bit of a time-out to serve your country. Hell, serve the world."

"It's just… very frustrating, sir," I gritted out.

"Yes." But he didn't say more than that.

We drove a few more hours then stopped at a Holiday Inn in a town I'd never heard of. I was pretty sure we were heading north. I thought maybe we'd passed Duluth and Grand Marais, but I wasn't sure. What I was sure of was that I was tired. Not just physically tired but soul-deep-exhausted-of-the-whole-situation.

Jacey looked the way I felt, a tight, miserable expression on her face as we entered the hotel.

I slipped my arm around her and kissed her hair as we waited for key cards to be programmed.

"I'd try to convince you two to split up and bunk with Hansen and me, but I know it would be a futile exercise," Bea said.

"You'd be right," I replied.

She sighed and handed us our key cards. "We'll be in the rooms on either side of yours. And here's a couple of panic buttons. Keep them on or near you at all times. Got it?"

"Yes." Jacey took one button, and I took the other. They were clearly meant to be worn, but I could only imagine Bea and Hansen rushing into the bedroom, guns drawn, because Jacey and I accidentally activated an alarm during a good, long, hard fuck.

And that was exactly what we were about to be doing, in my mind, anyway. I'd run it by Jacey, of course, but I thought she'd need the release as well.

"Bedside table?" Jacey whispered to me as Bea and Hansen flanked us and escorted us up to our rooms.

"You read my mind," I responded.

Hansen and Bea didn't leave us until we were securely in our room with the door closed and the safety latch in place. The room had two queen beds. But we'd only be using one.

"Baby, I want it hard and fast. How about you?" I asked, reaching out to pinch a nipple through her shirt.

She leaned into me and slid her hand into my pants, stroking my cock. "That sounds great. For round one."

"Fuck me, I knew I loved you for a reason," I groaned and kissed her.

HARD AND FAST

-Jacey-

I zipped open Caleb's pants and wrapped my hand fully around his thickening cock, pumping it for good measure.

Precum leaked out the tip. "Take off your clothes," he grunted, lust burning in his eyes.

With a smile I hoped came off as coy, I let go of his rigid dick and started stripping off my clothes, holding his eyes until I pulled my shirt over my head.

He grabbed me before my face cleared the collar and started rolling my nipples between his strong fingers, sending tingles to every part of my body. I felt myself getting wet for him. Well, wetter.

His cock rubbed between us, sliding against my stomach. His precum made our skin even more slippery.

Caleb unsnapped my bra after my shirt hit the floor. "Panties," he ordered, grazing his teeth up my neck.

I shivered and shimmied my panties off. "You, too."

He reluctantly let me go long enough to whip his shirt over his head and to divest himself of pants and boxers.

Then he was on me like an animal.

Caleb didn't bother with either of the beds. He lifted me onto the table-desk against the wall, kicking the wheeled office chair out of the way. "Spread your legs," he growled.

I did, and his long, thick fingers delved inside me. My fingers scrabbled against the wallpaper behind me as I let out a wanton moan.

He thrust his dick in me then, and it was so much bigger and better than his fingers. "Caleb!" I cried, grabbing his shoulders and arching my pelvis against his.

With another growl, he began thrusting so hard the table creaked ominously, even though its legs were thick and sturdy.

It was a very lucky thing for the hotel that they had the table lamp pasted firmly to the table's surface, because otherwise, like the remote control to the television and the welcome binder, it would have become a casualty of our passion.

I dug my heels into his back and held on, letting him rough ride me. It was fantastic. My ass squeaked on the tabletop, but Caleb's grip was strong enough to keep me right where he wanted me.

"I-I'm..." I panted, feeling the fireworks start beneath my skin.

"Come for me, baby," he said, picking up the pace just that little bit more that sent me over the edge.

I had to stifle a scream—our guardians were in the next rooms after all—and clawed Caleb's shoulders as my orgasm overtook me.

He grunted and began slamming desperately inside me, riding my orgasm until it brought him to his own. He grunted and bit his lip, stopping a cry of his own, and spurted his hot seed inside me.

My whole body trembled from the aftereffects of the pleasure he had given me, and I sat up properly, his dick sliding out a little, so I could wrap my arms around his neck.

Caleb kissed me hard, panting against my lips. "Baby, that was so good."

"It was," I agreed breathlessly.

"I don't know if I can move," he chuckled, still holding me against his body, keeping his cock from sliding out any further.

"There's no rush," I assured him. I laid my cheek on his sweaty shoulder and let my body melt into his, resting in the time I knew was between sessions.

In fact, he hadn't completely lost his erection. I could feel it.

"You know," he said. "Someday we should go back to Canada."

I blinked at him. "For real?"

"Yeah," Caleb replied. "We can find some other place to camp in the wilderness."

"You want to go fishing or something?" I asked, confused.

He laughed. "Not really. But I do want to fuck you until you scream your head off, and we're the only two who can hear it." He nibbled my neck, then soothed the spot with a kiss. "I want us to be completely free."

"That would be nice," I agreed. "But that's a long way off, I think."

Caleb shrugged. "It's nice to dream."

"It's a good dream." I ran my fingers through his sandy hair. It had grown out a bit since our time with the sheik. "I like your hair this long."

He smiled at me, his eyes glinting with good humor. "That's random."

I blushed. "Just an observation."

"Well, I suppose we're even, then, because I'd cry if you ever cut your hair," he said, playing with the ends of my hair which reached the small of my back.

"Then I won't. I don't want to see you cry," I murmured, brushing my lips over his.

Caleb deepened the kiss and moved his hips so I let out a moan. "Me neither, baby."

I WAS SLEEPING on Caleb's chest when the phone rang. I blinked my eyes open while he leaned over to pick up the hotel phone, a frown on his face. "Who would be calling at this hour?" he mumbled, glancing at the clock. It was 3:26 AM.

"Maybe Bea or Hansen asked for an early wake-up call?" I yawned.

He shook his head. "We're supposed to be staying here for a few days. There'd be no reason." Caleb turned his attention to the phone. "Hello?"

His face went absolutely white. "How did you find us?" he hissed.

I could hear enough from where I was to know it was Masterson. Even though I couldn't hear the words, I recognized the tone.

Caleb and I slapped our hands down on our panic alerts at the same time.

"Hang up!" I said, frightened, glancing at the curtain-covered window, the door.

He shook his head. 'Bea and Hansen,' he mouthed at me.

Speaking of our two protectors, I heard loud banging on the door and scrambled out of bed.

"Caleb? Jacey?!" Bea shouted.

Not caring about the fact I was still naked, I pushed back the door latch and wrenched the door open while Caleb stayed on the bed with the phone to his ear, stiff as a board.

"It's Masterson," I whispered desperately. "He called not five minutes ago. He's still on the phone!"

"Bea, close and lock this door, then call in a team," Hansen said. While Bea complied, he strode over to Caleb and pressed the speaker button on the phone.

"I'm assuming from all the white noise we're no longer having a private conversation, Caleb," Masterson tsked. His voice made my skin crawl. "That's disappointing."

"I guess you're just going to have to learn to live with disappointment," Hansen replied gruffly while Caleb set the receiver on the bedside table. We all could hear now anyway.

"Is that the FBI?" Masterson trilled, sounding far, far too happy for someone whose ass we were going to help nail one of these days. "How lovely. I assume this is Special Agent in Charge George Hansen?"

I could hear Hansen grinding his teeth. "You're very well-informed."

"You have to be in my business. And I suppose you're calling in a

SWAT team to move our little treasures somewhere else. Pity we didn't get them at the hotel," Masterson sighed.

"What can I say? Armored vehicles and bulletproof glass are the in things these days," Hansen grunted.

"And I suppose Special Agent Beatrice Kent is also there," Masterson continued.

"I wish I had your contacts. We'd have scooped you and the sheik up by now and sent you both straight to hell," Hansen growled.

Masterson tsked again. "Temper, temper. Well, I just wanted to say hello to the kids and maybe cause a bit of a stir."

"You are a motherfucking bastard, Masterson," Caleb snarled.

"There's the Caleb I know and love. But, consider this. If you're making me lose sleep, well, I think I'm well within my rights to return the favor," Masterson said.

I could just see him examining his nails in an aloof manner behind his desk, a smile playing on his lips. Masterson was enjoying every second of this. "Should we hang up?" I murmured to Hansen.

"Oh, Agent Hansen wouldn't dream of it," Masterson chuckled. "I'll bet he's recording me right now on his phone and planning to turn the recording in as evidence of witness tampering and harassment, blah, blah, blah."

"Aren't you already in enough trouble?" Caleb asked. "Why add fuel to the fire?"

"Dear Caleb. Because I can. Besides, I was watching some playbacks of the fun you two had while you were living here with me. Made me miss you."

Caleb bared his teeth, even though Masterson couldn't see him. I felt sick to my stomach. I knew exactly what he'd been watching.

"Masterson, I think we're done here. If you don't mind, we have a lot of maneuvering to do tonight, thanks to you," Hansen said. He hung up the phone before Masterson could answer.

Caleb grabbed the phone and tore it off the wood it was glued to, ready to tear it to pieces.

I hurried over to the bed and stopped him, taking the phone away and sitting in his lap. I slipped my arms around him while he took several deep breaths to calm down.

"Thank you, Jacey. We don't want to disturb the neighbors more than we already have," Hansen sighed.

"I swear, someone should just shoot him. Forget about the court case and everything. Just walk up and shoot the man," Caleb grumbled, hugging me back.

"I have those days, too, son," Hansen said.

"ETA fifteen minutes," Bea interrupted, still holding her phone to her ear.

Hansen began to pace. "How in God's name did he find us?" he muttered.

"I'd like that question answered before we end up getting killed at the next location," Caleb said. "You know, just for funsies."

"Believe me, son, I'm going to be working on that problem day and night until I've got it figured out." Hansen continued to pace. "Bea and I are both going to have to get new phones. They should be completely unhackable, but I am now having my doubts."

"Or you could be like us. Phone free is the way to be," Caleb suggested.

Hansen paused in his wearing down of the carpet, then nodded. "Yes. We'll have to do that."

"What does that mean for our safety?" I asked.

"Your panic buttons will still alert local authorities, and we can carry receivers on our person instead of relying on our phones," Hansen said slowly. "I also think we should stay mobile."

"So… we're sleeping in the car?" Caleb raised an eyebrow.

Hansen shook his head. "We're getting an RV."

DEPOSITIONS

-Caleb-

We got very comfortable in our RV. For months, Hansen drove the beast all over Minnesota just waiting for word that it was time for us to give our depositions.

I was pretty sure I had sex with Jacey in all of the ten thousand lakes. It wasn't exactly convenient to have us all in the RV when we were feeling frisky.

Jacey was lying underneath me in the sand on the beach of lake 10,001 while I thrust into her, both of us moaning in ecstasy, when Hansen called out loudly.

"It's time, kids. Finish up and come back to the RV. You're giving depositions tomorrow."

Breathing heavily, I still managed an, "Okay!"

Jacey spiked her fingers through my hair and cried out as her body trembled, squeezing my cock while she came.

I pumped her full of my cum then collapsed on her, panting. We were both going to need a shower to get all the sand off. Luckily, there was a shower in the RV.

While I wanted to rest there for a while, I knew Hansen would come find us if we didn't show up soon, so I reluctantly pulled out of Jacey and stood, holding out my hand to her.

She took my hand, and I pulled her to her feet. Sand trickled off both our bodies. I brushed some off her ass, holding her against me.

"Caleb," she giggled, leaning up to kiss my cheek. "Hansen's going to come down here any second. We need to get dressed!"

I gave a caveman grunt. "I could just carry you off into the woods and have my way with you."

Jacey laughed harder. "You just *had* your way with me."

I leaned down and kissed the shell of her ear. "It wasn't enough."

She shivered but gave my chest a firm push. "Don't you go getting me all hot and bothered, Caleb Killeen. Now, where'd you toss my dress?"

With a sigh, I let her wander off a little way to where I'd tossed her dress and went hunting for my own clothes. Jacey's panties were sticking out of my jeans pocket, but that was probably the best place for them, for now. She needed to get the sand off her before we could put those back on her.

I just had to live with the discomfort as I pulled my jeans up over my sandy body. I wore draped my shirt around the back of my neck, though. I didn't need to be itchy and chafing all over.

Jacey bounced back over to me in her sundress. She'd taken to wearing those, which I liked because it meant easier access for me. Honestly, I didn't know why she even bothered with panties.

"Okay. Let's go shower," she said, taking my hand.

"You know there's only room for one of you in that thing at a time, right?" Hansen grunted, and we both jumped.

"Hansen!" I griped, putting myself in front of Jacey before remembering she wasn't naked anymore. "How many times do I have to tell you to make some noise or something?"

"Sorry." He wasn't a bit sorry, and we both knew it. "I'm telling you, though. You break it, we're all going to smell pretty bad tomorrow at the deposition."

"Yeah, yeah," I grumbled. I tugged on Jacey's hand, and we followed Hansen back up to the camper.

Bea smirked at us as we went inside. "Did you kids have fun?"

"Always," I grinned while Jacey blushed. I kissed her neck. "You go ahead and shower first. I'll wait out here."

"Okay." Jacey headed to the back of the RV. Soon, I could hear water running.

Hansen sat down in the driver's seat next to Bea and swung around to face me. "You really ought to marry that girl."

"I will, just as soon as we're done running from Masterson, the sheik, and half the world." I flopped down in another chair. "You know, she should be going to college and pursuing her dreams. It really sucks that the only thing I can do for her is…"

"Screw her senseless?" Bea offered.

I winced. "Yeah, I guess."

"And love her with all your heart," she amended, patting my knee. "We're going to try to get you out of this mess. Hopefully, once the trial's over, there will be more we can do."

"After the trial's over, you're handing us over to Interpol," I reminded her.

Bea gave me a sympathetic look. "Yeah, I suppose that's true."

"Look on the bright side. You can screw her on every surface in Europe and maybe actually get married in Paris," Hansen suggested.

"Thanks," I replied sardonically.

"Anytime." He looked past me, and I turned around, seeing that Jacey was dressed in a new sundress and out of the bathroom.

I stood and walked over to give her a sandy hug. She swatted my chest. "Caleb! You're getting me all dirty again!"

"Getting you dirty is my favorite activity," I grinned, and she swatted me again.

"Go shower. I set out some clothes for you," she said.

I slid my hand down to squeeze her ass, then let go with a light peck on her lips. "I'll be out soon."

She rolled her eyes but still gave me a coy smile that went straight to my dick. "Don't be long."

"Yeah, don't be long! I want to get going," Hansen said.

"Yessir." I went and showered off the sand, wishing, for the millionth time, that the shower was big enough to hold two of us. After that smile, I wanted another round. Maybe two.

I came back dressed and ready to go. Hansen threw the RV in gear, and we started back down to the cities.

"It's about a twelve hour drive, so, you kids might want to go take a rest," he called over his shoulder once we finally reached a paved road.

We must have been somewhere near the Boundary Waters. At least, that was my guess.

"You could play checkers or chess," Bea suggested.

"We've done that," Jacey groaned, making a face. "A lot."

"Monopoly?" Bea offered.

With a pout, Jacey looked at me. "Caleb always wins. I think he cheats."

I theatrically put a hand to my chest. "You wound me! I would never!"

"Yeah, yeah." Jacey gave me a scowl then grinned.

"What?" I asked.

It didn't take long to find out 'what.' Sitting across from her at the table, half out of sight of Bea and Hansen, had been a very, very bad idea.

I felt Jacey's toes creep up the inside of my thigh then over my cock. She started massaging my dick through my jeans.

I gave her a warning look, but it was no use. She just smiled innocently while she rubbed my dick with the ball of her foot.

Stifling a groan, I gripped the edge of the table while she rubbed one out of me. I knew I absolutely destroyed my boxers when I came. I just hoped it didn't show through my jeans.

I was so getting her back for this.

But not now. Later.

There must have been something mischievous in my expression because she wagged a finger at me. As if that was going to stop me.

I locked my hands in front of me and twiddled my thumbs, signaling to her that her time was coming.

Jacey licked her lips in anticipation.

That one little gesture, plus the fact she was still making little circles with her toes, made me cum again.

"I'm going to go take a nap," I said, standing and quickly facing the back of the RV.

"Have fun," Jacey responded, though she pouted a little.

I frowned at her, and she still gave me an innocent look. Minx.

In the back of the RV, once I'd closed the dividing door, I changed out of my pants and boxers and put on a new pair of each. Then I flopped down on the bed I shared with Jacey and closed my eyes.

Sleep didn't come.

And didn't come.

And didn't come.

It should have come. Jacey and I'd had a very active afternoon. But all I could think about was the upcoming deposition. Would Masterson be waiting for us? Was this all going to be one big elaborate trap, and Hansen's and Bea's efforts were for nothing?

We still needed to make it to testify in court. How were we going to do that without putting ourselves right in Masterson's sights? Or the sheik's? Or whoever?

Hansen was right. I should marry Jacey. We should get married, go to school, and fuck like rabbits until she gave us a houseful of kids.

Well, probably fuck like rabbits afterward, too, but I wasn't counting that. I just wanted a nice, relaxed life with the woman I loved. Was that too much to ask for?

Instead, even if we *did* make it through all this mess in one piece, we were going to be looking over our shoulders for the rest of our lives.

I punched my pillow. It just wasn't fair.

"Caleb?"

I craned my head around and saw Jacey in the master bedroom doorway. "Hey, babe."

"Are you okay?" she asked.

"No." I patted the bed next to me and opened my arm so I could tuck her into my side.

She snuggled right in, turning to face me so our faces were just a breath apart. "What's wrong?"

"Everything," I said. "Everything's wrong. I'm... I'm just so worried we're not going to make it out of this okay. And... even if we do... our whole lives are going to be about hiding."

Jacey nuzzled my nose with hers. "We'll have each other."

"Yeah, but... how do we even plan for a family? Or live our lives? I want to go to school. I know you do, too, even if you haven't decided what you want to do yet. That's all part of the adventure. We should be able to be young and... I dunno... carefree together," I sighed.

"Well, that would be nice," she admitted. "But we just don't get to have it, I guess."

I stared at her. "You're not mad about that?"

"I am." She wrapped her arms around me. "I just try not to think about it too much. I try to be grateful for what I have. Which is you."

Though still frustrated, I managed a smile. "You're grateful for me?"

"Every day," she replied without hesitation.

I cupped the back of her head and curled my fingers into her hair. "I'm grateful for you, too," I whispered and gave her a long, passionate kiss.

POKING AROUND

-Jacey-

Hansen took the first shift driving through the night. Since we got the summons in the late afternoon, it was mostly going to be night driving, and he and Bea would be switching off.

That meant Bea was sleeping in the berth closest to the master bedroom, snoring away while I tried to sleep through it. I could tell from his breathing that Caleb wasn't asleep either.

Bea's snoring wasn't the only thing keeping me awake. Nervousness over the coming deposition, and the following trial, had me a complete mess on the inside, if I was honest. I was trying to stay positive for Caleb's sake, but his point about us never being able to have normal lives stuck with me. Would we have any children? Would that even be a responsible decision, given the danger we'd always be in?

And what about school and careers and stuff like that? I mean, I was still undecided about what I wanted to be, but I wanted to be something. And Caleb desperately wanted to be a doctor. Would we be able to do any of those things?

What I really wanted to do was cry, but I bit my lip to keep myself from sobbing. Caleb was wrapped around me. He'd be able to feel that.

Speaking of what Caleb was 'feeling,' he shifted his hand from my waist to my breast, thumbing my nipple through the shirt of his I was wearing as a kind of nightgown.

"Caleb..." I whispered, not sure if there was more warning or longing in my tone. "Bea's right outside. And it's not like that door is anywhere near soundproofed."

We'd never done it in the RV. It was just too crowded. And even though we had our own room with a sliding pocket door separating it from the rest of the vehicle, like Bea's snoring, noise carried. I thought Bea and Hansen liked it because then they could hear if something went wrong.

Caleb smoothed his hand back down to my waist, and I thought that was going to be the end of it, but then his hand went lower. He grabbed the hem of my/his shirt and dragged it up.

I knew I should have discouraged him. But if all he wanted was a little heavy petting, I figured that would be okay. It would distract us both from the snoring and me from my worries.

Sitting up, I held my arms up so Caleb could take the T-shirt off, leaving me in my panties. Then he pulled me back against his naked chest, cradling me between his legs while he reached around the front of me and fondled my breasts, sending little zings of pleasure all through my body.

I leaned back against his chest, letting him do what he wanted. Then he hooked my legs over his and spread them. I knew what he was going to do. I knew, and I didn't stop him.

He moved one hand down into my panties, the other still tugging at my nipple. "Don't make a sound," he whispered hotly in my ear as he cupped my mound then moved the fabric strip between my legs aside in order to touch me intimately.

How was I not supposed to make a sound? Especially when two of his fingers pushed inside me, and he started thumbing my clit while he finger-fucked me.

"Caleb..." I bit back a moan.

"Shhh." He took his fingers out right as I was about to come. I made a sound of protest in my throat.

He chuckled softly and kissed the back of my neck. I felt his knuckles brush against my ass, as well as the waistband of his boxers.

I knew I shouldn't let him keep going, but I was on fire, and my head was a mess. here was only one thing that could make it all go away. I arched back against him as he guided the head of his big, fat dick inside me, biting the inside of my cheek so I didn't cry out in pleasure.

"You're so wet for me, baby," he whispered, pulling my hips down so he slid in as far as he could go. I whimpered, and he covered my mouth with his hand. "Help me fuck you. You know what to do."

I did—and I did. I moved up and down on his cock while he cupped his hand around my front and worried my clit with his fingers. He kept his hand over my mouth, thank God, or we'd be giving Bea and possibly even Hansen something to listen to.

When I came, Caleb bit my shoulder to stifle his own grunt. But he kept going. He didn't cum.

It was only then I realized I was being punished for making him cum in his pants earlier that day.

I stopped helping, but this did not deter him, and frankly, I was glad it didn't. It just felt so good to not think about the future for a while.

He shifted us so I was on all fours. My body shook with the force of his thrusts and my own pleasure.

Caleb bit me again when he finally came, and I was, again, grateful for his hand over my mouth because I came at the same time, trembling as my orgasm washed through me.

We collapsed in a tangle of arms and legs. I panted. He panted.

Then the worried thoughts came rushing back, and I sighed, pressing my forehead against his shoulder.

He stroked my back. "Don't worry," he whispered. "I'm going to be there, too."

I decided I hadn't been fooling anyone. He knew I was just as scared as he was. "Caleb?" I said.

Caleb tucked my hair behind my ear. "Yeah, baby?"

"Once it's all done and we're settled, I'd still like to have a baby with you," I murmured.

He smiled, and his lips brushed against mine. "I'd like that, too."

BEA SMIRKED at us the next morning, and I knew the jig was up. "Have a nice night?" she teased.

I'm pretty sure I went as red as my Pop-Tarts' filling, but Caleb managed to keep a straight face.

"I have no idea to what you could be referring," he said blandly.

"Uh-huh. Just remember, you break it, you buy it," Hansen grumbled, joining us with a jam-smeared piece of toast on a plate.

"Oh come on, we weren't going *that* h—" Caleb began, then stopped himself. "I mean, what now?"

Bea burst out laughing. "You two are cuter than a bug's ear. Ah, to be so young and in love…"

"And at it like rabbits all the time…" Hansen added.

"It's part of the young and in love thing. Don't knock it," Bea scolded him.

"I'm not knocking it. I'm kind of jealous, actually. Been a long time since this old man could pull an all-nighter," Hansen chuckled.

It was official. This was how I would die. I'd die of embarrassment in front of two super-secret FBI agents.

Caleb rubbed my back. "We didn't want to wake you up with another rousing game of Monopoly."

Hansen snorted. "Probably would have been quieter."

I groaned.

"Funny, it sounded something like that last night," Hansen grinned. "But, in all seriousness, we do need to get you guys ready for your deposition."

"How does it work?" Caleb asked while I died a million quiet deaths.

"Lawyers from both sides sit in a room with you and ask you questions. It can last up to seven hours for each of you—" Bea said.

Caleb interrupted. "What do you mean 'for each' of us? Aren't we going in together?"

Bea winced. "No, Caleb. You each get deposed separately. But don't worry. All you need to do is tell the truth. Then you can't stumble over anything in court later."

"I mean, of course we're going to tell the truth," he sighed. "But I was hoping I'd get to be with Jacey."

Hansen shook his head. "That's not how it works."

"They want to see you first then Jacey tomorrow," Bea continued explaining.

"This is some bullshit. I don't want Jacey facing those vultures alone!" Caleb protested.

I wanted to cry. That's what I really wanted to do. A desperate fear wrapped itself around my throat and squeezed. But, Caleb needed to calm down. And I was the only one who could make that happen. I put my hand on his thigh and looked up at him with a forced, confident smile. "It'll be okay. We'll both do fine."

Caleb raised an eyebrow at me. Okay, so I wasn't fooling him at all. "You should have someone with you," he reiterated.

"It's not possible, Caleb. Let it go," Hansen said sternly.

Caleb whipped his head around, and his mouth opened to say something I was sure was going to be very counterproductive, if not downright insulting.

I tugged on his wrist, and he looked back at me. "Caleb? Please? It's just two days. We've got Bea and Hansen. We'll be okay."

A low growl emanated from Caleb's throat, but he finally hunched back in his chair with a loud huff. "Nothing had better happen to her," he warned Hansen and Bea.

"We'll do our best," Hansen replied.

"Oh, that makes me feel just fantastic," Caleb grunted.

Bea patted his hand. "We don't want to make any false promises. This is a risk. But getting Masterson behind bars, and then the sheik, is probably the only way to get your lives back."

"Or at least some semblance of a life," Hansen said.

"It's okay, Caleb. This is what's best," I chimed in.

"Nothing about this is okay. Nothing about this has ever been okay." Caleb shook his head. "I want you to know, this is all because your dad's a dick and I lost my temper."

I thought all the way back to when he and I took off from our campsite on the lake in Canada, where we'd been for the most innocent of family vacations. Camp. Fish. Roast marshmallows. Instead, we ended up lost in the woods in a murderous man's cabin. He chased us to Masterson's illegal logging operation.

And that, as they say, was that.

"It's not your fault. And I'd say Dad's paid the price," I said softly, kissing his shoulder. As far as I knew, Dad was still wheelchair-bound, due to Masterson, and would be for the rest of his life.

Sometimes it was easy to forget my father, stepmother, and our half-brother were all still stuck in Masterson's clutches.

"Do you think, once we testify, the cops or FBI or somebody will be able to go in and get our family?" Caleb asked, voicing my thoughts.

"I hope so," Bea said. "But it wouldn't surprise me if Masterson moves them somewhere we can't find them."

Caleb swore, not under his breath, but loudly.

"Let's try not to do that during the deposition," Hansen advised.

"Does this ever end?" Caleb finally demanded.

It was the question we were afraid of asking because we both knew the answer and it wasn't anything we wanted to hear out loud. Because out loud would make it more real, more final.

Bea swallowed. My mind screamed at her not to say it. *Please, no!*

"It doesn't, Caleb," she whispered sadly. "I'm sorry."

My tenuous hope, which had been in complete denial of the truth of the situation, shredded to pieces. I squeezed my eyes shut, trying not to cry, but tears leaked out anyway, streaming down my cheeks.

"You're never going to have a normal life," Hansen said, hammering the last nail in the coffin. "Not ever again."

Caleb was quiet and unmoving for a long time. Then he gathered me tightly to his side and leaned his cheek on my hair.

"Fuck," he murmured brokenly.

DISGUSTING DEPOSITION

-Caleb-

It might have just been my imagination, but I thought Masterson's attorneys looked oily. All seven of them. Not just in appearance, but in the way they smiled and shook hands and locked eyes on me as though they were big fish in a little pond, looking at me, the worm.

They ignored the presence of the Attorney General the moment they'd finished shaking hands with her.

"Caleb Killeen," the man I'd identified as the lead snake said to me, "we meet at last. You've been so difficult to get a hold of."

"That's the idea," I quipped back, meeting his eyes steadily. I wasn't going to let this jumped up old bastard intimidate me.

His lips twitched. He seemed to think my attitude was funny. "Well, at least we get to ask our questions now."

"Lucky me," I replied.

The lead snake chuckled, and his cronies added their own snickers from his lead. "Oh, I can already tell I'm going to enjoy this."

"If we could begin, gentlemen?" the Attorney General said in a clipped tone.

"Absolutely," the lead snake responded. "Go ahead, Ms. Jepsen." He looked at the Attorney General.

The court reporter sat off to one side behind a computer screen, fingers poised over a keyboard.

"We are here today..." the Attorney General gave the date. "... with Mr. Caleb Killeen. Mr. Rob Chalmers for the defense..." She rattled off the other names, but I was only concerned with Lead Snake Rob Chalmers. The rest were just window dressing. They weren't going to shake me. "... Mr. Killeen, do you swear to tell the truth, the whole truth, and nothing but the truth, so help you God?"

"I do," I replied.

"Please state your full name and address for the record," the Attorney General continued.

"Caleb Michael Killeen. Address... FBI custody?" I tried.

The Attorney General simply nodded.

"Excuse me," Chalmers said, his voice as slippery as an eel. "But if we don't have a permanent address for him..."

"Mr. Killeen is in special witness protection custody. As I'm sure you know, we've had some trouble keeping him safe. Therefore, if you need a permanent address for him, by all means, list it as this building because this is the only place you're ever going to see him outside of court," the Attorney General snapped.

I liked her a lot.

Chalmers held up his hands. "All right. I just wanted to be thorough. We wouldn't want there to be any reason to throw his testimony out in court..."

The Attorney General reeled back and struck like a mongoose. "As you well know, according to statute..."

The legalese she recited started to go over my head, but by the way the six lawyers next to Chalmers started sinking in their chairs, I got the impression my side was winning the sparring match.

It was annoying that Chalmers remained calm, but I suppose one can't have everything they want.

When the Attorney General was finished, he calmly folded his hands in front of him. "I see. Well, far be it from me to waste any more of your precious time, Ms. Jennings. In fact, why don't you go first?"

"Thank you, Mr. Chalmers. I will." The Attorney General turned to me. "Mr. Killeen, I'm sure you understand the seriousness of this deposition. I need you to tell the truth—to both of us. Do you think you can do that?"

"Yes, ma'am," I replied. I looked only at her, ignoring Chalmers' presence completely.

"Good. Now, you stumbled upon Mr. William Masterson Sr.'s logging operation last summer, did you not?" she asked.

God, had it already been over a year? "Yes, ma'am. By accident."

"And what did you learn about this operation?" she continued calmly.

"I was told within the first five minutes of meeting the workers that it was an illegal logging operation, ma'am," I responded.

"And how did you learn it was Mr. Masterson's illegal operation?" She looked at me expectantly.

I took a deep breath. "I found out when I was staying with him, ma'am. Mr. Hank Collins had just entrapped my girlfriend, Jocelyn Ann Collins, within his house, and my friend Will—William Masterson Jr.—helped me get her out and let us stay with him. We later learned we were being watched and recorded on camera, even during intimate moments..."

"You're getting a bit off topic, Mr. Killeen," Chalmers said.

I glared at him, but the Attorney General nodded. "Yes, Mr. Killeen. We will discuss all that later. For now, please tell me how you found out Mr. Masterson was the owner of the illegal logging operation."

"He told us, ma'am." I shrugged. "He told us, and then he trapped us into serving him, so I learned a lot more—"

"Mr. Killeen," Chalmers said again.

Now even the Attorney General was glaring at Chalmers. She gathered herself with a sigh. "Mr. Killeen, did Mr. Masterson kidnap you?"

"Yes, ma'am," I replied. "Several times."

"And he forced you to serve as an assistant to him in his criminal dealings?" the Attorney General asked.

"I was his personal assistant, yes."

The Attorney General nodded. "And in that capacity, what did you find out?"

I detailed everything in as organized a manner as I could, from Masterson's different areas of business down to the specifics and even the fact I was certain he'd had a whole container of people who'd been trafficked killed.

After a few follow-up questions, the Attorney General said, "Thank you, Mr. Killeen. Those were all my questions. Mr. Chalmers?"

I wasn't sure exactly how a man could appear to swagger while seated, but Chalmers somehow pulled it off. "Mr. Killeen," he oozed, "how old are you?"

Uncertain of where he was going with this, I glanced at the Attorney General. She nodded at me.

"I'm twenty-four, sir," I replied cautiously.

"And your girlfriend? Ms. Jocelyn Collins?" Chalmers pressed.

I frowned in confusion. "Jacey is almost nineteen."

Chalmers gave me a smile like the cat who got the canary. I was the canary. "So, you've been physically intimate with her?"

"Excuse me?" I blinked. "I don't see how that's any of your business."

"Mr. Chalmers?" the Attorney General asked.

"I have a point. I just need to get the facts in order first." Chalmers smiled at me and it made me feel like I needed a shower. "You're five, almost six, years older than 'Jacey,' aren't you?"

It wasn't a question. "I'm about five-and-a-half years older than her, yes."

"When did you first have sex?" he continued innocently.

I suddenly saw where this was going. "I didn't touch Jacey until she was eighteen."

"That's not what her father says," he revealed, his eyes twinkling with victory.

That sonofabitch. If Hank weren't already in a wheelchair, I'd be tempted to put him in one. Then again, he probably wasn't testifying of his own free will... "I've got a question for you, Rob. Are Mr. Collins and the rest of my family still in the custody of Mr. Masterson?"

Chalmers raised his eyebrows. "Mr. Killeen, I'll ask the questions here."

The Attorney General murmured, "Just answer his questions truthfully, Caleb. Let me do my job in the follow-up."

I took a few deep breaths, then said, "Hank is mistaken. I did not commit statutory rape, if that's what you're implying. I had sex with Jacey for the first time on the night of her eighteenth birthday."

"I suppose you can prove that somehow?" Chalmers laughed.

"There was a meteor shower that night," I grunted. This was so violating. That night was special—between Jacey and me.

Jesus, was he going to ask her the same disgusting things?!

"Oh, that's hard and fast evidence." He gave the Attorney General a sardonic smile.

"It's the truth. And you leave Jacey out of it. It's none of your damn business," I snapped.

Chalmers leaned forward, crowding me with his dark presence. I knew I should have been scared of whatever was going to come out of his mouth next, but right then, I was just pissed. "What would you say if I told you Mr. Collins has compelling evidence that suggests you were coercing Ms. Collins into a physical relationship with you *before* her birthday?"

"I'd say he's pulling a whole lot of nothing out of his ass because that didn't happen," I all but snarled.

"Caleb, you need to answer the questions as calmly and reasonably as possible. Just give the facts," the Attorney General advised me.

"In fact, there is photographic evidence of you being inappropriate with Ms. Collins a few birthdays ago," Chalmers crowed.

I couldn't even begin to fathom what that evidence could be, unless someone was getting creative with AI or Photoshop. "I don't understand."

Chalmers pulled out his phone and quickly pulled up a picture. "Explain this, please, Mr. Killeen."

I glanced at the picture but was still confused. "I'm hugging her."

"Mr. Collins believes you were touching her inappropriately in this picture," Chalmers said.

"By hugging her?" I still couldn't figure out what his problem was.

"He believes, what can't be seen in the picture, is you fondling her breast," he grinned.

I stared at him. "You've got to be kidding me."

"I'm not." Chalmers kept grinning at me.

"She's like fifteen in that picture. Of course I wasn't touching her that way," I protested.

"Mr. Collins says he can think back and see the signs all along. Were you not grooming Ms. Collins? Coercing her all this time?" he asked.

"No." I folded my arms over my chest. "Jacey had a crush on me, but I left and stayed away because she was far too young for any of that."

Chalmers chuckled. "But you wanted her, didn't you?"

In all honesty, I couldn't remember when I started wanting her. But it wasn't when she was fifteen, I was sure of that. Her clumsy confession had me spooked. I lit out of that situation like my tail was on fire. "I didn't want her then."

"When did you start wanting her?" he asked.

"I don't know," I replied honestly.

"Before her eighteenth birthday," he suggested.

That much… was… unfortunately true. I glanced at the Attorney General again, and she gestured for me to speak. "Yes."

"And when you say you 'didn't touch her,' did you do anything other than penetrative sex before her eighteenth birthday?" he smirked.

"I'm not answering that," I growled. "That's none of your damn business. I didn't coerce her. I never forced her to do anything or think anything or feel anything. Her thoughts and feelings are all her own."

"Do you really think that, Mr. Killeen?" Chalmers asked.

I nodded. "I do."

"And what would she do to keep you out of prison, do you suppose?" He was so smug, it radiated off him.

"Anything. And I'd do the same for her," I revealed without hesitation.

"How very sweet." The snake seemed to think he'd coiled himself around me, and all he needed to do was squeeze.

Better me than Jacey. "Are you done? Are you going to leave Jacey alone?"

"Oh, heavens no, Mr. Killeen. To both of your questions." He put the squeeze on, then. "Though, if you come clean about, say, your misdeeds that you tried to pass off on Mr. Masterson, I might not need to depose Jacey tomorrow."

"That's enough, Mr. Chalmers. Mr. Killeen was sworn in under oath. You have no reason to believe he has been anything other than truthful," the Attorney General barked.

He ignored her. "Mr. Killeen?"

It was tempting to take the fall for Masterson, especially since he was implying Jacey would be seen as the victim of my coercion and be allowed to walk free of all this. But there was still the sheik, and, well, it might have been selfish, but I didn't want to be apart from her for one day, much less the rest of my natural life. In prison. "Everything I've said here today is true. And you can tell Masterson to shove it."

Chalmers's expression darkened. "I see. I suppose you know, then, I will not be merciful tomorrow or in court."

"I suppose you know that could be construed as a threat," the Attorney General snapped.

"Could be. But it wasn't." He speared me with his evil eyes. "It was a promise."

"We're done here. Stop recording," the Attorney General said to the stenographer.

Chalmers and his team of cronies rose. "Tell Jacey I say hello. Oh, wait, you can't. You'll be separated until after her deposition."

I blinked, then turned to the Attorney General. "What?"

"It's common practice. We can't have you contaminating each other's testimonies," the Attorney General explained regretfully.

Chalmers giggled. The bastard *actually* giggled! "I guess you won't be able to warn her at all about tomorrow. Shame."

Rage turned my vision to red, then black. By the time I woke up, I was kneeling on top of the table and Chalmers had a split lip.

"I'm pressing charges!" he yelled, holding a handkerchief to his lip while the Attorney General dragged me back off the table. "I want his ass in jail!"

The Attorney General let out a long sigh. "All right. Caleb, you're going to have to spend at least one night in jail. I'll see what I can do for you from there on out."

I saw the smirk on Chalmers's face. He considered this a victory.

And I'd handed it right to him.

ALL BY MYSELF

-Jacey-

Caleb did not come to the hotel that evening. I was sure he would be rattled, and I was hoping we could comfort each other with our bodies. I was worried about my deposition the next day, after all.

"Where's Caleb?" I asked Bea and Hansen as the sun dipped below the horizon. "Is everything okay?"

The way they looked at each other made me think everything was *not* okay. But Bea pasted a smile on her face. "Sorry, we should have told you. Caleb's not allowed to influence your deposition, so you two can't be together tonight. You'll see him soon, though."

"Yes. Soon," Hansen echoed.

"How soon is soon?" I asked suspiciously.

They looked at each other again. "Well…"

"What happened?" I demanded.

Hansen rubbed the back of his neck. "Caleb got himself in a bit of trouble."

"What kind of trouble?" I asked, my chest going tight.

"He punched Masterson's attorney," Bea replied with a wince.

"He… did what now?" I gasped.

She shrugged. "We don't know the details, and even if we did, we wouldn't be allowed to share them with you."

"So, what does that mean? Where is he?" I asked.

The two of them sighed, then said together, "Jail."

"Jail?!" I shrieked, my voice at least an octave higher than a dog whistle.

They flinched. "Don't worry," Hansen said. "The Attorney General is already working on getting him out. All you need to worry about is your deposition tomorrow."

"Oh, so now I need to be *worried* about my deposition tomorrow?!" I started to pace. "And you're just telling me *now* I wasn't going to be allowed to see Caleb tonight? *And* that he's in prison?!"

"Jail," they corrected me.

"Whatever." I sat down on the edge of the sofa in our two-bedroom suite. "You just tell whoever's in charge that I won't give my deposition until Caleb's out of jail."

With a sigh, Hansen sat down next to me. "Jacey, if you start playing those games, Masterson's side is just going to use it against you in court later."

"It's not a game! None of this is a game! This is our LIVES!" I shouted, desperately looking around as though this may all have been some mistake, and Caleb would come popping out of a corner any time.

Bea knelt in front of me and took my hands. "I know. I know, lovey. But you really do have to do this deposition. The Attorney General might not be as inclined to help Caleb if you don't."

I wasn't going to cry. I wasn't going to cry. I burst into tears. "This is so unfair! We didn't do anything wrong, and we're the ones being punished!"

"Well, Caleb did sock a lawyer in the mouth..." Hansen pointed out.

"I'm sure he had a good reason!" I countered.

"Be that as it may, it landed him in jail," Bea said. "Actions have consequences."

"For us," I added bitterly.

"Just give your deposition tomorrow. Go along and get along and all that," Hansen said.

I glowered at him. "I'm tired of going along and getting along in every damn situation we find ourselves in. Everyone wants a piece of us. All the time."

"Jacey, just do as you're told. Tell the truth. Come back here. With any luck, Caleb will be here by the time you get back to the hotel." Hansen's words were clipped. He wasn't happy with my little tantrum, I guessed.

Tough.

"He'd better be," I groused and waved Bea off so I could get off the sofa and go to bed.

Of course, I didn't sleep.

What's going to happen now? was the question that plagued me for the rest of the night.

I DISLIKED Mr. Rob Chalmers the second I walked in the room. It might have been because of his puffed up presence. But mostly it was because he had a split lip and bruised skin around it, and I knew he must have been the one Caleb attacked.

Sitting down next to the Attorney General, I simply glared at him the entire time I was being sworn in. I wondered if the lady at the back recording the whole debacle was able to make notes like that: WITNESS STARES AT MR. CHALMERS AS THOUGH SHE WANTS TO STRANGLE HIM.

Mr. Chalmers was completely unfazed by my angry look, however. He just smiled at the Attorney General. I hoped his lip hurt like hell when he did it. "Ms. Jepsen, a pleasure to see you again."

"I wish I could say the same," the Attorney General grunted. "I don't suppose you've rethought your position on pressing charges against Mr. Killeen?"

Chalmers pressed a hand to his chest, his eyes wide and affronted.

Fake affronted. Anyone could tell that. "I take assault very seriously, Ms. Jepsen. As should you."

"I do take assault very seriously. And harassment. And threats. I'd suggest you be a little less... *you* today," the Attorney General muttered.

He laughed. "Oh, you are always so funny, Margerie. Now that Ms. Collins is deposed, I suppose we should get right to it."

The Attorney General ground her teeth, then turned to me. "Did Mr. William Masterson Sr. try to rape you, Ms. Collins?" she led in without preamble.

Chalmers's eyes just about bulged out of his head.

Good.

I raised my chin. "Yes, ma'am. Twice."

"I'm not comfortable with this line of questioning. Mr. Masterson is not on trial for rape," Chalmers objected.

"Neither is Caleb Killeen, but here we are. You threw that door wide open, Rob, so you stuff your objections," the Attorney General said.

"Wait, why would Caleb be accused of rape?" I asked, confused.

Chalmers gave an indignant snort. "We'll get to that later. Trust me."

"I don't understand," I said, looking at the Attorney General.

"Mr. Chalmers will enlighten you during his line of questioning. Unfortunately, I can't," she replied icily. The ice wasn't for me, though. It was for him.

I sat back in my chair, frowning at Chalmers. Whatever it was he was going to ask me, I wasn't going to like it. And if it was bad enough to make Caleb punch him, then I knew it had to be awful.

"Did Mr. Masterson force you to get pregnant by his son and carry that child to term?" the Attorney General went on.

"Yes. He took my son away," I said softly, my gut twisting.

"Did he?" she followed up her question with a second.

"Yes. He took Will away," I whispered.

"And now you're taking Caleb away from her by pressing charges against him when you were the one being verbally abusive. Great look on you and Mr. Masterson, by proxy, Rob," the Attorney General sniffed.

Chalmers turned red. "He assaulted me."

"You provoked him."

"I'm not on trial here!" he bellowed.

"Yet. Someday…." The Attorney General shook herself. "Never mind. You're right. You're not on trial here. Ms. Collins, did Mr. Masterson take footage of and watch you being intimate with Mr. Killeen?"

"Yes. I saw the footage myself when they left the door to the control room at the house open," I said.

"That would be Mr. Masterson's property on Lake Minnetonka?" she asked.

"Yes."

She nodded. "Those are all the questions I have for now. Mr. Chalmers?"

Chalmers drew himself up. "Ms. Collins. How old were you when you first started to 'have a crush' on Mr. Killeen?"

"I think I was fifteen," I replied, confused. "What does that have to do with anything?"

"And how old were you when Mr. Killeen started making advances on you?" he asked, ignoring my question.

A lightbulb clicked on in my brain. "I don't know," I lied. "But when that did happen, I was the one making advances on him."

He smirked at me. "Ms. Collins, you do know. Are you going to lie in court, too?"

"The second part is true," I argued.

"When?" he asked again.

"A day or two before my eighteenth birthday," I finally admitted. "And I did come on to him."

Chalmers snorted. "You wouldn't even know how."

"How very sexist of you," I snarked. "It was just a day or two. And we didn't do anything. Why does it matter?"

"I think he coerced you," he said. "I think he's coercing you now. I think he took a young, fifteen-year-old, starry-eyed girl and made her his unwitting accomplice."

"And I think you're delusional. He left when I was fifteen and I told him my feelings. He barely ever came back, and he avoided me like the plague," I replied. "And besides, I don't think he or I are on trial here. I do know a voyeuristic, murderous, rapey asshole who is, though."

His smile didn't waver and that made me very, very nervous. "Your father will testify that Mr. Killeen was grooming you from the time he married your stepmother."

"My father tried to keep me locked in my room and hit me when I refused to give Caleb up. He had no idea about us. Plus, he's under Masterson's control. Unless they live somewhere other than his estate these days," I scoffed.

"So you admit Caleb and you had something going on when you were younger," he pressed.

"I most certainly do not." I scowled at him. "And if you were asking Caleb things like this, I just think you're lucky he didn't break your jaw to get your lying, gross mouth wired shut."

Chalmers raised an eyebrow. "I think that might be construed as a threat."

"I think you're badgering the witness," the Attorney General said. "If you have nothing further, I think we're done here."

"Was it good, the sex with Will?" he asked, ignoring the Attorney General. "Did you have some threesomes? Was Caleb jealous?"

"You're disgusting." Bile rose in the back of my throat at the very idea of being with someone other than Caleb. It was bad enough I'd had my eggs harvested, and been used as an incubator, then had my precious baby ripped from my arms. "When this is over, and Masterson's in prison, I'm getting Will back."

He laughed. "I'd like to see you try."

"We're getting way off topic here. But, as the mother of the child —" the Attorney General began.

"She's not the mother. She was just the surrogate." He kept laughing. "And she was paid for her services, too."

The Attorney General looked at me. "Were you paid to be Will Masterson Jr.'s surrogate?"

I gaped at her. "You've got to be kidding me! Of course not!"

"I can prove it," Chalmers said. "There's an offshore account."

"That's great, but it's not mine." I looked from the Attorney General to Chalmers and back again. "I don't know what you're talking about! Masterson told me I'm Will's mother—"

"I think you're getting too upset to continue this today," he said in a smarmy tone. "Maybe we should stop recording."

"Hell, by how off the rails you've taken us, Rob, we might have to depose her again tomorrow," the Attorney General seethed. "Stop recording. I want to see what we have." She walked over to the stenographer.

Once she was distracted, Chalmers leaned across the table toward me. "You're nothing but a gold-digging whore."

I wanted to slap him so badly my hand tingled, but it wouldn't do any good for both Caleb and me to go to jail. It would probably only look bad at trial.

"Karma is going to bite you in the ass, Mr. Chalmers. It doesn't need any help from me," I said between my teeth. Then I spun on my foot and headed for the door.

The Attorney General looked up. "Ms. Collins, I'm not finished—"

"*I'm* finished. Until I get Caleb back, I'm done talking," I said. "I won't allow you to let him rot in prison just so this guy can ask if I'm having threesomes and call me a 'gold-digging whore.'"

"He did what now?" The Attorney General shot an accusing glare at Chalmers who tried to look innocent but was too satisfied with himself to pull it off.

"She did threaten me," he sighed. "But I suppose, in the interest of fairness, I should let that go. I did go a little off the rails there. We'll have to continue this tomorrow."

"Only if Caleb comes home tonight." I pushed open the door and walked out.

JAILHOUSE BLUES

-Caleb-

After a day in jail, or at least I thought it was a day, my cell door opened and another prisoner was shoved in.

"You're not the type to end up here," my cellmate said, eyeing me.

"I punched a lawyer," I replied, trying to sound big and bad. This guy was three times my size, and I wasn't a small man.

My cellmate snorted. "That'll do it." He extended a meaty hand to me. "Tyson."

"Caleb," I responded, shaking his hand.

Tyson blinked. "Killeen?"

My heart stopped. "Yes? My reputation precedes me?"

His gaze flicked around us, then he focused back on me. "You do know there's a hit out on you, right?"

I'm fucked. I looked at the guy who could bench press me and probably six tables to boot and swallowed. "I guess I do now."

"Pfft. Don't worry about me. You're in luck. I'll bet they threw you in here on purpose, thinking I wouldn't mind tacking on another life sentence or two to get a little money." He chuckled. He pounded me on the back, and I almost lost my balance. "But I don't kill people who don't deserve it. I mean, government does it, you're a hero. Guy who lives in a rough neighborhood and just wants to see the coke dealers stop peddling to little girls? He ends up here."

"You killed someone?" I asked. My voice didn't crack. Nope. Not one bit.

Tyson guffawed loudly. "Caleb Killeen, I've killed seventeen so far." He showed me some tattooed hash marks on his arm. "Planning to kill more if I get a good lawyer. Don't want that trash living around me and mine. But you're just some dumb kid who let a lawyer hassle him into getting sent here where you're a fish in a barrel, my man."

Yep, definitely fucked. "I'm sure the Attorney General is working on getting me out," I gulped.

"You stick with me, you'll get through this. Oh man, this is funny as hell. Okay, maybe not to you, but I think this is hilarious. They put you in with me. Morons," he said.

"You're offering to watch my back?" I asked, confused.

"I'm not offering. I'm telling you I'm going to," he replied. "You need it, kid."

"But... uh... sorry to look a gift horse in the mouth but... um... what's the cost?" I inquired. "It's been a crazy year for me, and it's become more and more important for me to ask things like that."

He inclined his head. "You have had a shitty year."

"Tell me about it," I sighed.

"Well, kid, I figure you're a whistleblower because you strike me as the boy scout type. What are you blowing the whistle on?" he asked.

It wasn't an answer to my question, but maybe he was just gathering more information. It wasn't anything I felt I needed to hide. Hell, if I got offed in here, maybe he could testify in my stead and protect Jacey. "It started out as illegal logging in Canada, but you know those big corporate bad-guy types. I drilled all the way down to human trafficking." I shuddered, remembering the call with the hired gun who killed a container full of people.

Tyson scowled. "I see. Well, I'm definitely not a fan of human trafficking."

"Arms. Drugs," I continued. "It's a guy named Masterson."

He sat down on a bunk and patted the spot next to him. "Tell me everything."

I plopped down beside him and gave him every detail, from Masterson's operations to the sheik's, to Jacey and my roles in the whole sordid mess.

Tyson nodded along, his hands balling into fists at points, but he didn't make any violent moves at me, so I just kept going, spilling it all.

Then I told him what happened that got Chalmers punched.

"He did that on purpose. You know that, right?" he informed me, shaking his head. "Kids these days."

"I didn't coerce my girlfriend." I folded my arms over my chest. "And if he keeps saying I did…"

"Don't go punching him again." He scratched the marks on his arm. It seemed like a force of habit. "You're deep in the shit now. I hope that Attorney General can get you out of here quickly. You've put yourself right in that Masterson guy's crosshairs. Maybe even that sheik's. And I don't know how long they'll let me stick around if I start protecting you."

I looked at him. "Why do you want to protect me?"

"Because, kid, you do the right thing. You could be living in the lap of luxury right now, serving one of those two bastards, but you're living in an RV on the lam. I'm sure you had other things you wanted to be doing with your life," he said.

I rubbed the back of my neck. "I wanted to go to medical school."

"See? You want to help people. And you're doing it anyway at great personal cost. That's what good people do. There aren't enough of those in this world." He stopped scratching his hash-mark tattoos. "They really missed the boat when they put you in with me, but they think all murderers are just crazy thugs who will do anything for a buck."

"You're cleaning up your neighborhood at great personal cost," I said quietly. "I can't imagine killing someone again, much less seventeen someones, but you're doing it and you're keeping kids safe. I don't see a black-and-white world anymore."

Tyson smiled. "Thanks, man."

There was a bang on the cell door and keys jangled in the lock. When the door opened, the guard looked surprised.

"He's not dead," Tyson smirked. "What do you think about that?"

The guard recovered himself. "Of course he's not dead. We don't just let people die in jail."

"He ain't gonna hang himself, either," Tyson continued. "Unless you and your friends want to become some tattoos."

Tyson's tone was enough to make *my* balls shrivel up and run away, and this was the guy protecting me. Being on the receiving end of that threat, I would have slammed the cell door shut and locked it and never come back.

The guard seemed to think he had some big, round, hairy ones though. He drew himself up. "I don't like your tone, Jones. I think I'll see if the warden wants to put you in solitary."

"I've met him. I don't think he's as keen on that hundred-million as you are," Tyson replied flatly.

"You watch yourself, Jones. I'll let it slide this time, but even a guy your size can be gotten to," the guard snapped.

Tyson wiggled his fingers in the air. "Ooo, I'm scared."

"Fuck you, Jones." The guard took several deep breaths to calm himself. "It's chow time. Off to the mess."

"Sounds good. You hungry, Killeen?" Tyson asked me.

I wasn't sure the worm was actually supposed to hop on the hook all by himself. "Uh… not really…"

The guard banged his nightstick against the doorframe. "It's not optional, Killeen."

"In that case, I'm starving," I said, rising. I also wasn't going to get myself in solitary confinement where God only knew what could happen to me. Likely me 'hanging myself.' *Fuck that shit.*

Tyson draped a heavy, yet companionable, arm around my shoulders. "Let's go."

"No touching. Jesus, Jones, you've been around the merry-go-round often enough," the guard tsked.

With a shrug, Tyson let me go but hovered very close. He put his big body between me and the guard, and every other guard we passed.

"How dead am I?" I whispered as we entered the mess hall.

A dozen eyes zeroed in on me as though I was a deer at a hunting convention. And they weren't just prisoner eyes, either.

"We're gonna try to make sure that doesn't happen," Tyson assured me. "Oh, by the way, don't eat the food."

"What?" I responded.

"They might try to poison you. Then you go to the infirmary and 'accidentally' die of food poisoning," he said.

Fucking great. "Fucking great."

"Don't worry. I'm not eating, either. Just push some shit around with your fork and dump it."

We both grabbed trays. I let them slop whatever they wanted to on it. It wasn't like I was going to be eating it anyway.

Tyson sat shoulder-to-shoulder with me at a long cafeteria table, his eyes narrowing on anyone, guard or prisoner, who came within five yards of us. It left several people pouting. But I was glad.

We both pushed food around on our trays and didn't eat a bite. I got up when Tyson did, but the big man walked behind me, not in front of me, as we brought our trays to the washing station.

"Good food?" the guy at the window asked sarcastically, looking at the swirls of slop on our trays.

"Fantastic. Best prison food I've ever had," Tyson replied with a grin.

The dishwasher grumbled and dumped our trays over the trash before throwing them in with the rest of the dishes.

I ignored my grumbling stomach as we were escorted back to our cell.

"It won't be for long," Tyson said, I guess hearing the grumbling as well. "You're a valuable federal witness. The Attorney General will get you out."

"Okay." I walked into the cell with him.

When the door slammed shut, I realized we weren't alone. Someone had been hiding behind the door.

"Jones," the newcomer said, sizing up Tyson.

"Erickson," Tyson replied to the man in a bored tone. Though I did detect a note of caution in there as he stood between me and a very thin, short man.

This led me to believe 'Erickson' had some skills that made up for his stature. I was sure I didn't want to find out what they were.

"You know he's worth a lot of money, right? I'll split it fifty-fifty with you," Erickson offered, examining his fingernails.

"I figure if I call the guards, no one's coming, right?" Tyson said.

"You figure correctly," Erickson responded.

"Hmph." Tyson sucked his teeth. "Well, problem is, Erickson, I have that pesky code."

Erickson rolled his eyes. "Don't go into the code again. I think I might have to tear my ears off."

"Code says you don't kill the good guys. You need a code, Erickson," Tyson said.

"Blah, blah, whatever. With a hundred mil, I can *buy* a goddamn code and spend time with it on my super yacht," Erickson snorted.

"If I could just say I'd rather not die, would that help?" I asked, not expecting much but feeling it was my duty to at least *try* to save my own life and save Tyson some trouble.

Erickson stared at me, poking my head out from behind Tyson's arm. "You… you'd rather not… die… you say?" He burst out laughing, holding his sides. "Damn, Jones, I know why you like the guy. Oh, that's damn funny."

Tyson shrugged. "He grows on you."

Erickson pulled a shiv out of nowhere. I think it might have been a toothbrush in a former life. "Time to remove the growth, then."

"I'm telling you, Erickson, you don't want to do that. He's gonna be testifying against human traffickers. He's needed. For the world," Tyson explained patiently.

"And I'm telling you, Jones, I don't give a damn." Erickson darted forward, quick as lightning.

Tyson knocked me back with his elbow, and I stumbled against the wall. He faced Erickson head on with his fists.

Erickson dodged and darted through Tyson's wide wingspan and stabbed him in the gut.

Tyson just grunted and kept going, taking several more stabs from the agile Erickson.

"Stop, stop it!" I yelled. "Leave him alone!"

"Ugh, you goody-two-shoes asswipes. You really think shouting at me's gonna stop me?" Erickson replied snidely, slicing Tyson across the cheek, just narrowing missing his eye.

"Fuck, you are such a pain in the ass, Erickson!" Tyson finally got a punch in, crushing Erickson's nose.

Erickson grunted and came back swinging with the shiv, slicing Tyson across the throat. "You should have taken the money," he said as Tyson grabbed his neck and gurgled.

"Tyson!" I darted away from the wall, not even thinking, as the big man went to his knees, bleeding profusely from his gut and from between the fingers of the hand he held at his throat.

Erickson smirked. The bastard actually smirked. "Now then," he said, turning to me as Tyson hit the floor, eyes wide and unseeing. "Where were we?"

Hate boiled over in me. I didn't care if I died now. I just wanted to do it wiping that fucking smirk off that asshole's face.

"Number Eighteen," I growled and launched myself at him.

REBELLING

-Jacey-

"Did you really say you wouldn't testify unless Ms. Jepsen gets Caleb out of jail?" Hansen asked, eyeing me as I sat in the back of the car on the way back from the disastrous deposition.

I folded my arms over my chest. "I did."

"And didn't I tell you that would be a bad idea?" he continued, frowning in the rearview mirror.

"I don't care." I hunched my shoulders like a mutinous teenager being called to task by her father. Well, I supposed, at nearly nineteen, I was a mutinous teenager. But Hansen was not my father. I actually respected him more.

Bea rubbed her temples in the passenger seat. "Jacey, Caleb did assault Masterson's lawyer."

"So? I wanted to assault him, too. But I also knew that was what he wanted. Which tells me he wanted Caleb to assault him. Which makes me think there's something unpleasant waiting for Caleb in jail, so it's very, *very* necessary to get him out ASAP."

Hansen looked at Bea, and I realized they'd already come to that conclusion.

"You've got to get him out *now*," I insisted.

"We don't have the power to do that. Not now that he's under the Attorney General's purview," Bea sighed.

"Then she's got to get him out now. Or she's down two witnesses, because I'm not rewarding her for screwing all this up. It was her job to keep Chalmers in check. She didn't," I argued.

"Jacey, the Attorney General can only do so much. Her hands are tied by the law," Hansen began to lecture me. "Whereas Masterson and his attorneys, well, their whole motto is 'as long as we don't get caught.' You hear what I'm saying?"

I glared at him in the rearview mirror. "I don't care if you have to go in there with a whole SWAT team, or whatever the FBI's equivalent is. You all need to get your poop in a group and get him out."

"I promise you the Attorney General is working as hard as she can —" Bea tried.

"She's not working hard enough, or Caleb would be here with me," I complained.

"Let's just go back to the hotel and talk about this like adults," Hansen sighed.

I shook my head. "We are talking about it like adults. You just don't like what I'm saying. You can take me wherever you want—restaurant, hotel, whatever—but I'm not going to agree to do another deposition or testify in court until I know for sure Caleb is safe."

"What if something happens to Caleb in jail?" he asked, broaching the subject head-on. "If you don't testify, you could be charged as an accessory to Masterson's dealings, or even the sheik's."

"Don't threaten me." I scowled at him. "Without my testimony, and Caleb's, Ms. Jepsen and INTERPOL have no cases. None. Nothing. So what you could make me an accessory *to*, I have no idea."

"Caleb would want you to save those human trafficking victims, if you can," he said.

That was a low blow. Of course, I knew Caleb would want me to keep going and testify if something happened to him. But I was me, not just an extension of Caleb. And if these people failed to protect him after all their promises, I wasn't going to feel particularly talkative anymore. I was tired. I was sick and tired of all of it.

"If something happens to Caleb, then I'll just have Will. And Will is currently in Masterson's care. Ergo, I will have to swallow my pride and go crawling back to that bastard in order to be with my son," I replied.

Bea's head whipped around. "You wouldn't."

"Try me," I growled.

They looked at each other again.

"Well, Bea, I think we have ourselves a problem," Hansen said.

"A loose cannon," she agreed.

"Whatever. You tell Ms. Jepsen what's at stake. Maybe she'll feel more motivated," I suggested.

Bea took out her phone. "Hi, Amanda. Is she in? Thanks."

I waited, one eyebrow raised.

"Ms. Jepsen?" Bea said. "We have a serious problem."

I listened hard. I wasn't going to let them buffalo me. She could be talking to static, for all I knew.

But I could hear enough of the Attorney General's response to recognize her voice, if not her words.

"Jocelyn Collins is refusing to testify in court, or give another deposition, unless Caleb gets sprung from jail." Bea held the phone away from her ear as incoherent shouting filled the air. "Yes, ma'am. I know he punched Masterson's lawyer. But we're all pretty convinced that was a staged provocation in order to put Caleb somewhere Masterson can get to him. And I think you're thinking the same thing."

There was a long pause.

Bea pulled the phone back and held it out to me. "She wants to talk to you."

I took the phone. "Yes, Ms. Jepsen?"

"You do know you've made a deal to testify, right? That the only way your own crimes go away is if you do testify?" the Attorney General reminded me.

"I was never charged with any crimes, but if you feel you have to, go ahead. All I hear is you dragging your feet over getting my Caleb home." My tone was icy. I felt ice all the way to my soul. I doubted

Ms. Jepsen had lifted a pinky to help Caleb. That made me suspicious of her.

"Ms. Collins, you have to understand how this works…" she started her own lecture.

"No," I interrupted. "You have to understand how *this* works. I am not doing one goddamn thing for you until you get Caleb out of jail. End of conversation. I don't care how you have to do it. I don't care what favors you have to call in. I don't care if you have to give out new favors, or if it looks bad for the trial, or if Chalmers has nude photos of you with the President of the United States. I don't care. You're trying to win a career make-or-break case. So all you have to ask yourself is if you're willing to march out of that courtroom after making an embarrassment of yourself because you were unable to provide witnesses. Or maybe it won't even go to trial at all, and you'll have the humiliation of failure hanging over you that way. I don't care. I only care about Caleb."

"He landed himself in jail himself, Ms. Collins," the Attorney General shot back.

"And that makes him an idiot. But he's my idiot, and I want him back." I was rather proud of myself. My voice didn't waver one bit.

Ms. Jepsen made a sound of frustration. "You're being unreasonable."

"You're wasting time. Tick-tock. Tick-tock." I stabbed the 'End' button.

"You know, Jacey, you're quite scary when Caleb isn't around," Hansen grunted as Bea took her phone back.

"Sometimes, I have to protect him, too," I replied fiercely.

"I think I'd kill to have the kind of loyalty you two have," Bea said, pocketing her phone.

Hansen frowned at her. "I'm right here."

"No offense," she told him, "but you'd leave me high and dry to save our country. Jacey's willing to watch the world burn to get Caleb back."

"That's what being young and stupid is all about," he grumbled.

"I prefer young and in love, but whatever you guys want to call it," I said.

We turned into the hotel parking ramp. After parking, Hansen and Bea got out of the car and flanked me on either side to the elevator.

When we got to our suite, the door was ajar.

Bea halted me with a hand on my shoulder. Hansen drew his gun and approached the door slowly.

Then he kicked it open. "FBI! FREEZE!!!"

A loud shriek and a thud accompanied his order, and he stepped into the room, his gun pointed straight ahead. "Get up," he said to someone I couldn't see. "Tell me what happened here."

The reply was a babble of terrified Spanish.

"Wait here," Bea said. "I have to go translate. If you see anyone, *anyone*, you call for us, you got that?"

I nodded. My heart was pounding. After Bea entered the hotel room as well, I pressed myself to the hallway wall, looking up and down the corridor.

A flicker of movement at one end, then the loud bang of a gun inside the hotel room, had me running into the suite.

"Oh no," I whispered, shaking as I saw the woman I knew was part of the Trinary standing over Hansen's body. She was wearing a hotel maid's uniform, but I recognized her just the same.

"Jacey, get out of here!" Bea yelled from her position behind the couch.

I looked at Bea, then at the woman, then back at Bea. Then back at the woman. I held up my hands. "You want me? Leave Bea alone," I said, my voice shaking. "Obviously the money's too good to pass up. Was it the sheik? Masterson?"

"Both." The woman grinned at me. "And why would I 'leave Bea alone'? I have you either way, and one less witness..." She turned and shot through the couch.

Bea grunted, then hit the floor, gripping her chest.

I did the only thing I could think of. I turned and ran.

"Tsk, tsk, tsk. Ja-a-cey," the Trinary woman said. I heard another shot and then just knew that Bea was dead. But I couldn't think about that now. "J-a-a-cey..." echoed down the hall.

I didn't look back. I kept running, slamming through the door to the stairwell. I wasn't getting trapped on an elevator. That would be a real rookie move.

Of course, TRI-nary meant there were another two of them around, and one of them smirked at me as I reached the level below. I yelped and turned on my heel, pelting up the stairs.

"You know, they did say it could be dead or alive," he called from down the stairs. "You might as well stop running!"

"Fuck you!" I shouted back without so much as turning my head. I couldn't get distracted. Not now.

I had to get away.

I took the stairs all the way to the roof, my lungs burning as I burst through the door. The third had to be around there somewhere. On the ground. On the roof. Somewhere.

Unfortunately for me, on the roof was where he was. He came out from behind an industrial air conditioning unit and pointed his gun at me.

"You need to give up now, Ms. Collins. It's over," he said.

The door behind me creaked open, and I knew the other two were at my back.

"Did they say dead or alive?" I asked, my words coming out in a wheeze.

"They did indeed," the female Trinary member said.

I swallowed. *Caleb, please be okay.* "Then it's going to have to be dead."

As they closed in on me, I dashed to the edge of the roof.

And jumped.

LUCK BE A LADY

-Caleb-

The shiv stabbed into my shoulder. I shouted in pain, but as Tyson had said, no help was coming.

And no help came.

"You are such a pain in the ass, you know that, right?" Erickson grunted, thrashing underneath me as I took him to the cement floor. The shiv stabbed over and over again into my back as he struggled to get out.

At least he couldn't see what he was doing or else I might have gotten a punctured lung. Or worse.

I gritted my teeth against the pain and squeezed my hands around his throat, crushing down on his larynx. If I was dying today, I would take him with me.

Jacey, please be okay.

The shiv finally stabbed something important—maybe a kidney?—and my hands loosened. I collapsed on the bastard.

"... Where are the guards? What's going on?" a female voice filtered through the cell door.

"Ma'am, you can't go in there," one of the guards said.

My vision swam.

"... Go wherever I damn well please. Now open this door!"

I recognized the voice, but I was too far gone to really take it in.

The shiv twisted in the angry spot it had found. "Be a good boy and die now, Killeen. I'm afraid play time's over," Erickson said.

The door scraped open.

I blacked out.

I WOKE up in a hospital room.

"Christ..." I groaned, my body aching.

"You almost went to meet Him," the Attorney General said, getting up from a chair in the corner of the room and coming to my bedside. "Fortunately, they were able to save your kidney."

"What about Tyson?" I asked.

She grimaced. "I'm afraid he was too far gone."

Sadness weighed down my chest. "He was a good guy."

"He was a serial killer," she snorted.

I glared at her. "He saved my life and probably the lives of a lot of poor little kids."

"Fine." She shrugged. "You think what you want about Tyson Jones."

"I will." I looked around. "Where's Jacey?"

"Her deposition didn't go as planned. I'm afraid you won't be able to see her until she gives a second one," the Attorney General said, but there was something behind her eyes I didn't like.

I locked eyes with her. "Where are Bea and Hansen?"

"Just fine." She gave me a smile.

It wasn't a very convincing smile. "You're lying to me."

She sat down on the edge of my bed. "Look, Caleb, there are a lot of things going on that even I didn't know about. It's made things very difficult..."

"Where are Bea, Hansen, and Jacey?" I demanded.

"Caleb..."

"Excuse me, ma'am? They just told me Bea didn't make it," an officer, who I was sure was trying to be helpful, said, poking his head in the room.

The Attorney General winced. "Thank you, Seth."

"And Hansen?" I asked before the officer could leave.

"Oh, he didn't make it away from the scene. He died right on the spot," Seth said sadly.

I nodded, waited for Seth to leave, then rounded on the Attorney General. "Where is Jacey?"

She fiddled with my blanket. "Well, what you have to understand, Caleb..."

"I'm not going to understand a damn word out of your mouth until you tell me what the FUCK is going on!" I shouted.

She glared at me. "Listen here, you jumped up little shit—"

"Am I interrupting?" a smarmy voice I recognized did, indeed, interrupt.

Now she turned on Chalmers. "*You* aren't supposed to be here!"

"A man's not allowed to bring flowers to a sick patient anymore?" he asked innocently.

"No. Especially if it's you. Beat it," she said.

"Hmm. Mr. Killeen, do you want me to 'beat it'?" He smirked at me.

I wanted to destroy the bastard, but at least he might give me some answers. And letting him in would piss off the Attorney General. She deserved it at this point. "Come on in."

"Thank you." Chalmers came in and set a large bouquet of lilies on the ledge by the window. He pulled the chair the Attorney General had occupied while I was unconscious closer, then sat down in it himself. "Exciting few days."

"*Few* days?" I repeated. "How long have I been out?"

"Just three days. You'll be fine, they tell me. I'm so happy for you." He did, in fact, look almost gleeful, which told me the information I was seeking was going to be very bad indeed.

"What happened to Bea and Hansen?" I asked.

"Rob, leave the boy alone. He's had a very traumatic experience," the Ms. Jepsen inserted quickly.

He shook his head at her. "Now, Margerie, you know you

shouldn't tell lies to your witnesses. It makes them so touchy when I expose those lies on the stand. Or need I remind you of the Altier case?"

She turned beet red.

"Chalmers, go ahead. Dig out your pound of flesh. What happened to Bea and Hansen?" I asked again.

"Why, it was the most tragic thing," he said, his voice dripping with false sympathy. "They were on protection detail for your precious Jacey, and someone shot them both in the suite you were all staying in. Terrible business."

I nodded, deliberately not looking at the Attorney General who was waving her hands and shaking her head at Chalmers. "And Jacey?"

"They chased her to the hotel roof, and she jumped." He was trying, and failing, not to sound positively giddy.

Everything went into slow motion. I couldn't breathe. My heart stopped. "What?"

"We haven't found a body," the Attorney General said quickly. "So there's every possibility—"

"That she grew wings and learned how to fly?" Chalmers finished sardonically. "She splattered herself on the roof of a truck or tanker. Some farmer's going to find her in his flatbed. Whatever happened, she's dead. No one could survive a fall from that height."

The Attorney General's nostrils flared. "No body," she repeated. "And the camera only showed her jumping. There are no witnesses saying they saw her hit the ground."

"Like I said. Truck. Splat," he replied.

I jerked up, not quite involuntarily but at least before I thought about it. The sharp pain that accompanied my move had me lying back down immediately. A couple of monitors shrieked. "If it is the last thing I do…" I hissed at Chalmers. "I am going to *end* you."

He just laughed. "Son, it's over. You can't even take care of your-self. We all know you're never going to make it to trial. Think of losing Jacey as your wake-up call." He stood and patted my knee before heading for the door, walking out just as a nurse rushed in.

"We don't know she's dead," the Attorney General said again as the nurse fussed over me.

"Will you *please* stop upsetting my patient! Oh hell's bells. Help me turn him on his side." The nurse snapped her fingers at her.

Her eyebrows hit her hairline, but she did as she was told, helping the nurse to roll me. The nurse harrumphed loudly. "Just as I thought. Pulled some stitches. Now I have to go get the doctor." She stabbed a finger at the Attorney General. "You stop riling him up."

"I didn't!" she protested.

The glower on the nurse's face made her amend, "I was trying not to."

"Try harder." The nurse stormed out.

"Before the doctor gets here," I wheezed. "I want to know what you think."

She blinked. "Pardon?"

My chest went tight, but I forced the words out. "Do you think Jacey is alive?"

"I... I don't know what to think," she lied.

I nodded slowly. "So you don't think she made it, either."

"Caleb..."

"Just go. I need to think about some things," I managed. I turned my head to the window.

The Attorney General sighed and rose from the edge of the bed. "She'd want you to testify."

I gripped the sheets in my balled fists. "Just GO!!!"

She winced but made her way out.

My eyes stung, but I forced myself not to cry. I couldn't break down. Not yet.

The doctor came in a moment later and looked me over.

I was wheeled to imaging, and after that, I was wheeled into surgery, only this time, they didn't need to put me out to fix the damage.

Then, I was wheeled back.

The world still turned.

That was how I knew Jacey had to still be alive. It wasn't desperation on my part. I just knew, if she had died, my world would have ended.

Instead, it kept trudging along.

All I needed to do was find out what happened to her.

She was fine.

Jacey was fine.

She had to be.

SOMEWHERE OUT THERE

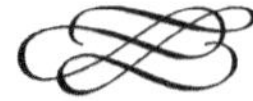

-Jacey-

"Honey, I don't think you belong here," a low voice drawled.

I blinked my eyes open. Was I in Heaven?

Heaven sure smelled bad.

I tried to sit up, but my bones hurt too much to let me. The last thing I remembered was jumping off the top of the Holiday Inn Express.

Maybe this was hell?

A stubbly face came into view. "What are you doing in a great big pile of manure?"

Manure? I tried to sit up again, but my ribs really hurt, my arm, a leg, for that matter. It was burning in my eyes, so I blinked several times to clear them.

Did I land on my side?

Wait, I landed somewhere other than the sidewalk?

I was alive?!!!

"I..." I croaked. "I... jumped."

"Oh honey, life can't be all that bad. Was it a bridge?" the man asked after a pause. "We're gonna have to get you to a doctor..."

I shook my head as vehemently as I could without aggravating, well, everything. "No doctor. I'm… I'm running away from some bad people. If I go to a doctor, they'll find me."

"So, not a suicide attempt, then." The man stroked his chin. "Didn't anybody tell you jumping off things could get you killed? What were you jumping away from?"

"I jumped off the Holiday Inn," I replied. "The roof. There were people up there trying to kill me."

The man gave me a sympathetic look. "Seems we're gonna need to take you to a different kind of doctor, too."

It took only a moment for me to realize what he meant. "I swear I'm not crazy. I'm a protected witness. Except the people we're testifying against keep trying to kill us!"

"Should I be calling the cops, then?" the man asked.

"No. No! For all I know, he's paying them, too." I didn't know what to do. I didn't want to trust this man, but I could barely move, and he was all I had at the moment. "I know this sounds like one big mental conspiracy theory, but this guy, Masterson, we found out he does human trafficking and a lot of other bad stuff. He's been paying people to try to kill us so we can't testify in court. I swear I'm telling the truth!"

The man stared at me for a long moment. "Who's 'we'?"

"My boyfriend and me. Well, I mean, we'd be married now if it weren't for everything that's going on…. It's complicated." I felt miserable, not just because of whatever injuries I had but also because Caleb was in danger. Probably worse danger than me.

"You can't be more than twenty. What do you want to go and get married for?" the man scoffed.

I frowned at him. "Is that really the point right now?"

He held up his hands in surrender. "All right. I get you. I don't want to move you—Lord knows what injuries you might have—but I'll call a friend. He's a veterinarian. We'll get to the bottom of this. Oh, and my name's Billy, by the way. What's yours?"

"Jacey," I said. "And thank you."

"Not a problem. It's not every day I get involved in my own spy movie," Billy responded, shaking his head. "You sit still so you don't hurt yourself more."

"Okay." As Billy walked away, I focused on being as still as I could be.

That was until a state trooper in a wide-brimmed hat poked his head over the top of my manure crater. I saw the somewhat pointed roof of a barn afterward. "Well, I'll be damned, Billy. You weren't kidding."

"I said I wasn't. This little filly says her name is Jacey, and she's a protected witness, but there's a whole bunch of people trying to kill her. She jumped off the Holiday Inn when I was driving through the city. Can you believe that?" Billy said.

I started trying to squirm my way out of the manure. I needed to get away!

The state trooper looked at Billy. "Jacey Collins?"

"She didn't tell me her last name," Billy replied with a shrug.

"Oi, stop squirming around until Horace gets here. Though I still think we should probably take her to a hospital," the state trooper mused. "I'm Officer Jake Alexander. I'm not gonna hurt you."

"People tell me that all the time." I grunted, but I did stop moving around, mostly because I wasn't getting anywhere.

"Pretty sure they do." Officer Alexander actually stepped up into the truck, getting his boots covered with manure. "Everybody's looking for you. Mostly for your body, but this is a nice surprise."

I snorted. "What? Didn't you hear the ransom was dead-or-alive?"

"I'm not interested in any ransom," Officer Alexander said. "They say you're going against a man who's involved in drugs, arms dealing, human trafficking, and that kind of crap. I'd rather my kids grow up in a world where you can't get away with that kind of shit than become a corrupt cop and sell you out. Not even for a hundred-million dollars."

Billy gave a low whistle. "Dang, Jacey. That's a lot of zeros."

"Don't worry about Billy," Officer Alexander went on kindly when the blood drained from my face. "He wouldn't even know what to do with a hundred-million dollars. If he wanted to be rich, all he'd have to do is sell his farm to developers."

"They haven't offered me a hundred mil, but I'd be plenty comfortable, I can tell you that," Billy said. "But I like my life the way it is."

Huffing and puffing began to fill the air, and Billy and Officer Alexander looked off to the side. "Horace, you fat bastard. You finally made it," Officer Alexander joked.

"Yeah, you glorified meter-maid, I did." Horace panted. "Speaking of which, I'm missing a great big bowl full of strawberry fluff for this, so you'd better tell me what I'm doing here. What's in the manure?"

"You'd have to see it to believe it." Officer Alexander offered him a hand up.

Horace, indeed a rather rotund man, was then looking down at me. He wiped the sweat out of his eyes, then looked again. "Isn't that the girl on TV?"

"It is," Office Alexander said. "What they don't say on TV is whoever's after her killed two seasoned FBI handlers."

"She jumped off a hotel roof. Thank the sweet Jesus it was only five stories," Billy added. "And Lord only knows how she ended up landing in *my* truck while I was hauling manure. That's got to be some kind of miracle."

"I'll say." Horace knelt down next to me. "She isn't a horse, though. She should go to a real hospital."

"Why? So I can get killed trying to protect her? No thanks," Officer Alexander said. "I swore I'd be willing to die in the line of duty, but I'd rather keep that as a last resort."

Horace sighed. "I was afraid you'd say something like that." He turned to me. "I'm going to start looking you over. I'll tell the other two to go if I need to take off any of your clothes, okay?"

"Okay," I responded cautiously.

"I suppose someone put a lot of money on your head," Horace mumbled absently while he carefully began to examine me.

"Yeah. A hundred-million reasons to do bad things," Officer Alexander said.

Horace blinked. "Damn. Okay. Good thing I'm not hurting for money, then. I'd almost be tempted."

"Your fat ass couldn't catch a snail, much less a full grown girl," Billy snorted.

"Another reason I'm not tempted." Horace frowned as he got to my injuries. "Well, that's broken. I wouldn't be surprised if your ribs were cracked. And that leg's at least fractured. I need to take her back to the clinic for some X-rays."

"Is it okay to move her?" Office Alexander asked.

"Yeah. Mind the arm, but otherwise, she should be able to be carried." Horace stood back and looked at Officer Alexander and Billy expectantly.

Officer Alexander ignored the manure that surrounded me and scooped me up, handing me down out of the truck into Billy's arms while I whimpered with pain.

"Really ought to go to a hospital," Horace grumbled, but he seemed resigned to the situation.

"Not an option right now. Okay, so, Billy, lay her down in the back of the squad," Office Alexander said.

Billy took me to the trooper car and laid me down in the back. The cage between me and the front of the vehicle really rattled me, and I started struggling again.

"Woah, there. Calm down. It's just how squad cars are made." Officer Alexander interceded quickly, pushing Billy out of the way so he could gently pat my ankle. "No problems here. Just taking you to the vet."

I took several deep, calming breaths and squeezed my eyes shut, forcing the cage out of my vision. All the times I'd been trapped had risen to torment me, but breathing helped them recede. "Okay."

"Okay," Officer Alexander repeated.

Horace got in the passenger seat, and then we were off.

Every bump in the road, and I was sure the first part of it was gravel, made me groan. I tried not to, but I was in a lot of pain, though apparently not enough to blessedly pass out.

Still, it wasn't long until the squad car stopped, and Officer

Alexander carefully scooped me out. "We're here. Just want to make sure no one sees you." He put his jacket over my face.

I heard three sets of footfalls and decided Billy must have come as well.

Then I heard a door swing open with the tinkling of a bell. "Peggy, take the rest of the day off," Horace said.

"What's going on?" Peggy asked.

I was sure it was probably obvious to Peggy what was 'going on,' seeing as there was a covered, clearly human form being carried in, but I understood her incredulity.

"Just go. I don't want you involved in this if there're any consequences," Horace said.

There was some scuffling, another jingle. Then someone locked the door behind us.

A zip-zip-zip filled the air, then Horace gave a long puff. "All right. Blinds are all closed." The jacket came off my face. "Bring her into the back," Horace said.

What followed was a series of painful, but necessary, exams. Apologizing profusely, Horace carefully cut my clothes off so he could treat me properly. Officer Alexander stayed because I said he could, but Billy waited in one of the doggie exam rooms.

In a couple of hours, my arm was set—a thoroughly unpleasant experience—and wrapped in a make-shift cast. My leg was put into a brace that fit okay except for being a little short.

"It's Peggy's," Horace explained. "Good thing she left it here."

He also wrapped my ribs and filled up a paw-printed pill container with pain medication. "Don't go undoing my hard work. You need some rest. Are we keeping her at Billy's?"

"Can't think of a better place right now," Officer Alexander said. "At least not until I can figure out who's safe to contact about her. That's gonna take a while."

"Is Caleb okay?" I asked. "Someone has to make sure Caleb is okay."

"Her boyfriend," Officer Alexander told the other two. "And I'll check in. So far, he's in the hospital. There was a kind of incident at the jail."

I groaned. "I knew it. I knew Chalmers provoked Caleb on purpose!"

"He's got to rest. Just like you," Officer Alexander said. "I'll let the right people know you're okay. As soon as I figure out who they are."

"Maybe the Attorney General?" I suggested.

"Maybe." He sounded uncertain. "I want to look into that more, though. Somebody knew where you were staying. Somebody told whoever's after you. Frankly, I don't trust anybody."

My throat went dry at the idea that the Attorney General could be in on it. Was that why she didn't shut down Chalmers's disgusting line of questioning? Was that how Bea and Hansen got killed?

"Can you please check on Caleb?" I asked. "I just don't think the hospital is the safest place for him."

Officer Alexander grunted. "Neither do I."

WE GO TOGETHER

-Caleb-

I was sleeping when he came in. It was a good thing, too, because if I'd been awake, I would have hit my call button.

Or tried to strangle him with the cord

As it was, Masterson's voice had my eyes flying wide open the moment he began to speak. "Hello, Caleb."

I looked up at him and felt around for my call button, but the bastard had taken it off the bed, and now it dangled uselessly over the side where I couldn't even reach the cord. "Asshole," I hissed.

"Yes, yes, I know. I just wanted to come and personally give my condolences on your loss. Poor Jacey. If you'd only just stayed with me and done my bidding, everything would be fine. But no, you had to be a hero." He sighed.

"This is witness tampering," I reminded him. "And don't say her name. I don't want to hear it coming out of your filthy mouth."

Masterson chuckled. "Jacey. Jacey. Jacey."

I struggled to sit up, but I was still in too much pain. More pain than I had been in before, actually.

"You know, those damn morphine pumps, you can't ever rely on them. So touchy," he grinned, and I glanced at the pump. Sure enough, he'd lowered the dose to zero.

"Glad you're enjoying this," I grunted. "But I promise you, I am sending you to hell. I'm only more determined now." *They haven't found a body*, I told myself. I'd been telling myself this over and over through every sympathetic look I'd gotten from the Attorney General, guards, detectives, everyone.

"Life is full of little pleasures if you know where to look," he said. "But, as I'm sure you know, I have an ulterior motive in coming here. Since Jacey is roadkill…"

I shot up at that, and he took a surprised, cautious step back from the bed. I instantly regretted my move, however, and couldn't follow it through.

He smirked. "… Since Jacey is roadkill, I thought you might be more concerned about the rest of your family now. You can still save them."

"You can still let them go," I shot back. "The best way I can save them now is to put you in jail and pray that some big guy named Bubba makes you his bitch."

He threw his head back and laughed. "Even if I did go to jail, people like me go to Club Fed, not Sing Sing."

"We'll see, won't we?" I said.

Masterson sighed. "You are such a stubborn little shit. Well, there is another way for us to both get what we want. In fact, I'll be doing you a favor."

"Oh? How's that?" I asked.

He slipped a syringe out of his jacket pocket. "You can die. Then I won't need your family, and you can go be with Jacey."

Fuck. I looked around for something, anything, I could do. "You're a sore loser, Masterson."

"Silly Caleb. I never lose." He uncapped the syringe.

"Something tells me that's not antibiotics," a new voice drawled.

Masterson whirled around, dropping the syringe. "Who the —?"

A state trooper stood in the doorway of my room, leaning casually against the door frame. "Actually, I'm pretty sure you're not supposed to be here at all."

"Officer…" Masterson began.

"Alexander. Officer Alexander," he said.

"Officer Alexander, I'm not sure what you think you saw…" Masterson continued, recovering his convincing nature. "But I assure you—"

"Yeah, yeah. No, I don't want money. Yes, I know the syringe is going to disappear. Yes, I do expect you're going to have fifteen of these nice hospital staff testify that you were never here. Yes, I'm sure the cameras are even now malfunctioning. Just go, asshole."

Masterson drew himself up to his full height. "You're going to regret not taking money."

"I'm sure I will. Now get going." Officer Alexander folded his arms over his chest.

Masterson snatched the syringe off the floor, re-capped it, then strode out.

The officer barely made room for him to pass.

"Are you my new guard?" I asked him. "Because it doesn't seem like my old one liked his job very much."

"He's probably halfway to Bermuda." He walked over to my bed. "So you're Caleb Killeen."

I nodded. "That's me."

"She said I should come check on you. Good thing I did. Seems you can't stay here," he sighed. "I'm just trying to think if I should check you out AMA or if I should just steal you out of here and let them all try to figure out what happened."

"You did say the cameras were off. The Attorney General asked you to come check on me?" I asked.

He shook his head. "No. Jacey did."

I blinked at him. "They found her?! Is she okay?!"

"She's a bit banged up, but she's fine. And as far as finding her, she's not officially 'found,' exactly. We're all hoping to avoid the kind of problems you almost just had," he explained.

"Oh. Okay. Can you take me to her?" I asked.

"That's the idea. In fact, since the cameras are down anyway, I think I'll just wheel you on out." He walked back out into the hall briefly then came back in with a wheelchair. "Horace can get you some pain meds once we get where we're going, but for now, you might just have to grin and bear it. Looks like that asshole turned off your drip, too."

"I can do anything. Just get me to Jacey," I said.

He started disconnecting me from my various wires and feeds. When a monitor started to blare, he turned it off.

It still flagged someone, because all of a sudden, there was hospital staff at my door. "What do you think you're doing?" a doctor demanded.

"Getting the patient some fresh air. Why, you want me reporting that your cameras are down, and you let someone try to come in and kill him?" Officer Alexander asked sweetly.

The doctor turned red, and the staff around him paled. They'd clearly been waiting to come collect my body.

I scowled at all of them. "I'm leaving. Go fuck yourselves, and I hope it was worth it."

"Mr. Killeen," the doctor began. "I think you're under the mistaken impression—"

"I'm not mistaken about anything. You all can go to hell. In fact, I'm pretty sure that's right where you're headed at the end of your days," I snapped.

Meanwhile, Officer Alexander finished disconnecting me and carefully put his arms under my knees and the back of my head. "This is gonna hurt like a sonofabitch," he warned me.

I gritted my teeth and nodded.

The pain was, indeed, excruciating, but I kept Jacey on my mind and in my heart as he transferred me to the wheelchair. If I could just soldier through the pain, I'd see her soon.

"I must protest your actions. The patient is unwell," the doctor said stiffly.

Officer Alexander tucked a sheet around my legs. "Move," he simply replied, eyeing the staff.

Those who were at least moral enough to look shamefaced at their actions stepped aside while the doctor and two others blocked the door. "You're not taking him," the doctor argued. "You—"

Officer Alexander took his taser off his belt. "Who's first?" he asked.

The remaining three looked at the taser, and even the doctor got out of the way.

"Billy," Officer Alexander called as we approached the door. "Watch my back."

A man in a flannel shirt appeared out of nowhere, staring the gathered hospital staff down while Officer Alexander wheeled me out.

Staff here and there stopped to watch, openmouthed, as Officer Alexander wheeled me through the hospital, but no one else got in our way.

I kept my teeth dug into my lip to stifle any sounds of pain.

"Don't you worry, kid. Horace has the good stuff," Billy assured me from behind us as we walked.

"Who's Horace?" I managed to ask.

"Veterinarian," the men said together.

The pieces started falling into place. "Jacey was treated by a vet?"

"A really good one, too. No hospital records. No one knows she's even alive," Officer Alexander assured me quietly.

We got to the parking lot, and I saw a state trooper's squad car. I also saw the Attorney General walking up toward the door. When she saw me, she stopped in her tracks.

"Caleb Killeen, where do you think you're going?!" she demanded.

"Ma'am, there's just been an attempt on his life. Respectfully, he's going where you can't find him. You name the day and the time, and he'll be in court, but there's no way he's going back in there," Officer Alexander said.

The Attorney General gaped at us. "An attempt... court... what?!"

"Oh. We've got Jacey Collins, too. Don't try to find them. You'll be sorely disappointed," Officer Alexander informed her.

Her eyes widened. "You have... I don't... but... deposition!"

"There won't be any more of that, either. They each gave one, as far as I know. If you couldn't keep them civil and on track, that's on you," Officer Alexander grunted. "Now, if you'll excuse us."

"I most certainly will not!" the Attorney General yelled.

"Tough." Officer Alexander, Billy, and I shouldered past her. "Get ready for some more pain, Caleb."

I braced myself as Billy opened the back door of the squad car. Officer Alexander carefully picked me up and laid me inside.

"I want to see your badge," the Attorney General said, coming up beside the squad car.

"It's good to want in life," he responded. "If you need anything, call the state police. I'll get the message one way or another." Then he gently, but firmly, pushed her aside.

Billy returned the wheelchair to the hospital entrance, then walked past the bewildered Attorney General to get into the passenger seat. "See you later, ma'am," he said.

"But…"

Officer Alexander threw the car into gear, and we sped away, leaving her in the dust.

It was a very uncomfortable ride to wherever we went, and I didn't ask where we were going because I didn't want to know. I didn't want there to be any possible way I could betray Jacey's location, just in case Masterson pulled some sort of stunt on our way there.

Luckily, we got to our destination without incident. As far as I could tell from my laid back position, we were on some kind of farm. I could see a silo and part of the top of a barn. That and the excruciating dirt road we went down were sort of clues.

Officer Alexander parked, then came to get me. "Last time. You're doing great, Caleb." He picked me up with a strained grunt, and I didn't make a sound, but it was damned difficult. I wanted to scream.

Billy walked ahead of us and unlocked the front door of a quiet, unassuming white farmhouse. "Take him to the back. Figure they've probably shared a bed by now. Might as well let them go on sharing one. Then they can both be on the first floor."

"Good idea," Officer Alexander said. He carried me through the farmhouse, past the kitchen and a cozy little TV room, and stopped just shy of a large back porch. Billy opened a door on the left, and Officer Alexander sidled through with me.

"Took you long enough," an overweight, balding man grumped from beside the bed. "Thought I might have to sedate her."

I looked over and saw Jacey, bruised and with a casted arm, but alive, lying on the far side of the bed.

"Jacey…" I breathed, and my whole world shifted back into focus. Gravity returned. Everything was okay again.

Her lower lip trembled. "Caleb." She burst into tears.

"Be real careful. Maybe just hold his hand," Office Alexander warned her as he settled me down on the bed next to her.

She wrapped herself around my arm. "Caleb, I was so worried."

"Don't worry. Masterson only tried to kill me once," I quipped. "Okay, maybe twice if you count jail…"

She smacked my ribs, and I drew a sharp breath, but at least it was above my kidney. She winced, but still said, "It's not funny!"

"They told me you jumped off a building," I scolded her. "That's not funny, either."

"It was the Trinary! I didn't have a choice," she replied miserably. Her breath caught. "Bea and Hansen are dead."

My heart sank. "I know, baby."

"Caleb, when does this ever end?!" she wailed, and I wished I knew what to tell her.

"After the trial," Officer Alexander said firmly. "If I have to, I'll disappear you both myself."

PLAYING HOUSE

-Jacey-

As the months passed between Caleb's and my rescues and the trial, it was easy to fall into a new routine. A quiet, easy routine. As we healed under Horace's watchful eyes, we started being able to help Billy out more. He taught Caleb and me how to milk cows and collect eggs. Then, when we were both healthy again, we began mucking out stables and using a pitchfork to drop hay down from the hayloft to feed the horses below.

"You're the best farmhands I've ever had," Billy said over breakfast one morning as Caleb and I cooked together, insisting Billy sit down and just let us wait on him. "Maybe Jake will settle you right here after the trial. It's not like anybody'd look for you here." He sounded hopeful.

"We'd have to go into town eventually, and there's been a BOLO out for us already. Hell, we've been on TV," Caleb reminded him, pushing the bacon strips around a cast iron skillet. They sizzled and hissed.

"I hate to break it to you, but that BOLO went out *everywhere*. So did the news. I don't even know if it'd help for you to leave the country," Billy pointed out.

I groaned. "That's good to know."

"See? You might as well stay here," Billy said.

Caleb looked at me. "Well, it's not a terrible idea.… Who would look for us here?"

"Nobody. I'll talk to Jake about it. Heck, it's a big house. My grandma had eight kids. If Masterson lets your family go, they could come here, too," Billy suggested.

I shuddered at the idea of being under the same roof as my father. "I… uh… suppose…"

"If he hits you again, I'm dropping him off the top of one of the silos and calling it an accident," Caleb grunted.

"How would he have gotten up there in his wheelchair?" I asked.

"The power of prayer?" Caleb grimaced. "Okay, so, maybe he rolls into a river or something."

Billy laughed. "Before you go planning to murder your father-in-law, Caleb, maybe give him a chance to apologize? He should see how good you two are together."

"He had a chance to see that. He was still an asshole," Caleb muttered.

I finished frying the eggs for all of us, bumping hips gently with Caleb. "We can give him another chance. Billy won't let him stay if he's just as bad as he was before."

"I'll help you push him into the creek," Billy offered. "Just not until you give him another chance."

Caleb heaved a heavy sigh. "Fine." He finished the bacon, and I began plating the food while Caleb made toast.

Officer Alexander walked in then with Horace in his wake, neither of them knocking. That didn't really seem to be a thing at Billy's house. What was a thing was saying 'good morning' when you came in. But both Officer Alexander and Horace looked grim.

"What?" I asked, my heart pounding. "Did someone die?"

"Okay, maybe it's not-so-bad news," Horace murmured to Officer Alexander.

"What's the bad news?" Caleb asked, tossing some toast down on a plate. He glanced at me, and I fired up the burners again, preparing to make more food for the newcomers.

"Trial's finally coming up. Two weeks. The Attorney General reached out to the state police," Officer Alexander explained. "I sent a message back that you'd be there, but I've said it, and I'll say it again: you don't have to. You've already suffered more than two people have the right to, and the Attorney General, hell, not even my own boss knows where you are. I can just make you go away. It'll probably work just as well as testifying to get your family away from Masterson, and you won't be walking into his crosshairs."

I looked at Caleb. Caleb looked at me. Then I shook my head. "We have to testify. Especially for all those people whose lives were lost getting us this far."

"I told you they wouldn't take the easy way," Billy said, sounding proud.

"We're all going with you," Horace added, taking a seat at the table. "Is that bacon I smell?"

"Make another pound of it, Caleb. Horace is going to hog it all," Billy chuckled.

"You'd better believe it," the vet replied.

I got more plates and silverware out. While Caleb took care of the eggs and bacon, I poured orange juice and coffee for the newcomers then went to make more toast after setting butter and jam on the table.

"You're very brave, you two," Officer Alexander said, sitting down as well. "I just hate to drop this on you after everything."

"We knew it was coming eventually," Caleb replied. "I guess I'm just happy it'll be over. I mean, then we go to INTERPOL and testify against the sheik..."

"No, you don't." Officer Alexander's tone was firm.

Caleb looked up. "What?"

"You heard me. You're doing all the duty you need to. You don't have to keep walking from pillar to post so everyone can get their pound of flesh. They can take depositions if they want, but you're not being trucked all over the world for this bullshit," Officer Alexander said.

"We discussed it," Horace mumbled around a mouthful of toast. "Jake was in Camp Testify for a while, a long while, but then he came around to reality. You're both going to be a hundred by the time this ends. Eventually, someone else has to carry the ball."

"But…" I began, confused.

Officer Alexander interrupted me. "It's great you want to do what you can for the world. But it's going to be impossible to keep you safe the whole time. I don't know the people they're going to hand you off to, and I can't go with you. That sheik is just going to pay someone to kill you. I'm positive, after all these murder attempts. They can just take a deposition and use it in court. And this is the twenty-first century. If they need you to testify, they can do it remotely. No more of this bouncing you around the globe."

"They can stay here," Billy said hopefully.

Officer Alexander gave that some thought. "Well, here's as good a place as any. At least I'll be able to keep an eye on you."

"Great!" Billy was excited, and so was I. I looked over at Caleb, who grinned.

"I guess it's decided, then. You're going to have two really good farmhands for life," Caleb smiled.

"That's wonderful, and I'll pay you more than room and board once we get this all worked out, for sure," Billy added. "Can't have you all poor and needy. Work is worth a paycheck."

"Witness Protection will take care of that. We just have to give them an account to send money to," Office Alexander said. "They sure as hell owe you two."

Caleb nodded. "That works."

"But they'll be working for me. Surely I should pay you guys something," Billy argued.

"No," Caleb and I said together.

"You're doing us such a great favor letting us stay here," I continued. "If anything, we should be giving you hazard pay for keeping us."

"Hmph." Billy didn't seem happy about the money situation, but he didn't argue any further.

Caleb cleared his throat. "Just to let you know, Jacey and I intend to get married and have kids. We'd really like to go to college, but I can see where that might not be possible. I… wanted to be a doctor."

"You can come help me at the vet's office," Horace suggested. "I'll teach you everything I know. I know it's not human medicine but… well, I guess you never know, right? I never expected to be treating two humans, but here I am."

Caleb gave that some thought. "That actually sounds kind of neat. I like animals, and I'd be able to help out more around here if they get sick."

"Don't you go putting me out of a job, though!" Horace teased.

"Wouldn't dream of it." Caleb laughed.

"I kind of like farm life," I said, looking around at everyone. "It's nice here. There's plenty to do, and everyone helps out."

"I'd still understand you being disappointed about not being able to go to school," Billy responded sympathetically.

My smile wavered. "But I don't even know what I'd like to be."

"It's still a shame not having the full college experience," Horace said. "Frankly, it's not fair."

"It's not," Caleb agreed. He rubbed my back. "But that doesn't mean we can't still have a full, happy life."

'I love you,' I mouthed to him.

He smiled and kissed my temple. "Love you, too," he whispered in my ear.

"Aww, you two are cuter than a bug's ear," Billy sighed. "Doesn't look like I'm getting married anytime soon. Probably end up leaving the farm to you and your kids."

"Billy!" I gasped. "Oh my God, that would be more than generous! Don't you have extended family?"

"All of them would just want to sell it to developers," Billy snorted.

"Oi, is the bacon burning?!" Horace asked.

Caleb turned quickly back to the stove and started slapping bacon and eggs on plates. He then piled bacon high on a separate plate.

"That one's mine, right?" Horace asked, indicating the bacon plate.

"It's a miracle you haven't had a heart attack by now. You know that, right?" Officer Alexander said.

Horace stared in disappointment as I set a plate of bacon and eggs in front of him then set the plate of bacon in the middle of the table. "I'm fit as a fiddle," he insisted.

"Uh-huh. You kiss your wife with that lying mouth?" Billy chuckled.

"Hmph." Horace started on his bacon first.

Once we were finished making all the toast, Caleb pulled out a chair for me, and we sat down at the table as well.

"Eat up. Lots of chores today," Billy told us, biting into a piece of toast.

"He says it like it's a threat," Officer Alexander grinned. He began cutting his fried eggs up.

Horace reached for the bacon, but I pushed it back. "Not until you've finished your eggs," I scolded him.

He rolled his eyes. "Yes, Mother." He grumbled while he ate his eggs.

Caleb chewed on a piece of bacon right next to him, and Horace gave him a baleful look. "Good stuff," Caleb said.

"So, you two are okay with not testifying against the sheik?" Officer Alexander asked.

"Like you said, it's the twenty-first century. If they want our testimony that bad, they can ask us to Zoom in or whatever," I said. "I like it here. I want to stay."

"That's what I like to hear," Billy smiled. "Speaking of which, it's your turn to muck out the stables."

"What is it with you people and getting me all covered with manure?" I joked.

Horace snorted. "First time, you did it to yourself."

"Hmm. Yeah, I keep forgetting that part." I looked around at all of them. This felt like a real family.

A sudden stab of terror shot through me. Did that mean this was going to be taken away from us as well? Was it only a matter of time?

Oh God, are these people going to get hurt because of us?!

"Stop thinking so hard. You're going to give yourself an aneurysm," Horace grunted, finishing his eggs and giving Billy an expectant glare.

Billy pushed the plate of bacon down toward Horace. "I know you're scared," he said to me kindly. "But Jake's got this. We're all going to be okay."

It was as though they could read my mind.

Caleb dropped his chin onto my shoulder. "This time, we'll all get it right, baby. This time, it really will be okay."

"You don't know that for sure," I whispered.

"*I* know it for sure," Officer Alexander said. "Now eat up before the taskmaster here makes you go mow the back forty as well."

"I have a tractor!" Billy objected.

"Your dad didn't," Officer Alexander muttered. "Let me tell you, twenty-five bucks was not nearly enough for that bullshit. I think I have a permanent back injury."

They kept bantering, and my nerves settled. After all, it couldn't always go wrong.

Could it?

THE NIGHT BEFORE

-Caleb-

Two weeks passed faster than I expected. Faster than I wanted, for sure. Jacey and I spent days working hard on the farm, though I left middays to help Horace at his vet clinic.

"You've gotten some more muscles," Jacey observed one evening when she and I were making dinner in the kitchen.

That just brought to mind the fact we hadn't been intimate since our injuries. I wasn't sure which one of us was more scared of breaking the other one.

I looked around. Billy was still watching television in the living room. I put my hand on her ass and squeezed gently. "Do you like muscles?"

She gasped and almost dumped the whole pot of spaghetti sauce she was warming up. I grabbed the handle before it fell. "Caleb!"

After righting the pot, I put my hand right back where it had been. "I asked, do you like muscles?"

Jacey blushed as red as the sauce. "Yes, I like your muscles."

"Has somebody been watching me muck out the stables?" I went on with a grin.

She turned even more crimson. "Maybe."

I leaned in and nuzzled her neck. "Does someone… miss me?"

Jacey melted into a puddle of goo, leaning back against me, her eyes closed. "Maybe."

"Just maybe?" I nibbled her ear.

"Caleb, be good. We have to make dinner," she whined, though her whole body was telling me exactly what I needed to know. It had been far too long. For both of us.

"You know I'm good, baby," I whispered.

She swallowed, and I remembered just how good that throat felt around my dick. "Why are you getting so… uh… frisky… now?"

"Because you like muscles." I wrapped my arms around her and kissed her shoulder. "So we're gonna have to blame this one on you."

"Blame what on who?" Billy asked.

Jacey yelped and started stirring like she was a blender. "Nothing! Nothing."

I glanced over at him and saw him giving us a knowing smile. "Make a noise, will you?"

"And have you all ruining my grandma's kitchen counters? I don't think so," Billy joked.

"We'd never!" she gasped, looking at him as well. "Oh my God, Billy, not in your kitchen!"

"I don't know, I was thinking about it," I mumbled.

She swatted me with the spoon, getting spaghetti sauce on my arm. "Cheeky!"

Billy burst into loud guffaws. "You two are the best. Most entertainment I've had in a long time. Better than *Jeopardy!*"

"Glad we can entertain you," I grinned.

"Caleb. The noodles," she said.

I looked at the potato pot that was nearly boiling over. "Right." I reluctantly let her go. "I suppose we can have dinner first."

"Not too much. Not as much fun on a full stomach," Billy teased.

"'Girl Survives Several Assassination Attempts. Dies of Embarrassment,'" she quipped.

"I can think of better ways…" I began.

Jacey swatted me again. More spaghetti sauce clung to my shirt.

"You work on those noodles, mister, or we won't be exploring any 'better ways' tonight!"

"Oh, I very much doubt that," I said, using my low, sexy voice.

"Okay. Fine. So it'll probably happen anyway, but we're getting dinner on that table, Killeen," she scolded me.

"Yes, baby. Whatever you say." I checked the noodles and saw I'd almost let them get overcooked. I quickly dumped the pot out into a colander in the sink.

"Better check the garlic bread, too," Billy said, starting to set the table.

I sniffed the air, and Jacey jumped aside to let me get to the oven. "Still good!" I responded after pulling back the foil. The edges were just starting to get a little black, but the bread was mostly nicely browned. I took it out and plated it.

"I think the sauce is nice and warm. We should be ready. Salad's in the fridge," she said, setting the small pot of sauce down on a trivet on the table.

I rinsed the noodles with hot water, tossed them a few times in the colander to get the water off, then dumped them in a bowl with tongs and set the bowl on the table.

Billy got the salad and a variety of dressings.

"Ready to testify tomorrow?" he asked after we'd all gotten our food on our plates.

I choked. Jacey pounded me on the back. "You don't ever mince words, do you, Billy?"

"Nope," he replied. "I kind of figured you two were nervous, and I thought we'd talk about it."

"Not a lot to talk about, I guess," I said, taking a swig of water. "We're going there. We're testifying. I mean, hopefully they get to our testimony tomorrow. It's bad enough we're going to be out in the open, but I'd hate for anybody to follow us back here."

"Jake thought of that. Won't give you the details, but suffice to say, if you don't get called tomorrow, he's got somewhere for you to go until you do get called," Billy assured us.

Jacey breathed a sigh of relief. "Oh thank God. I don't want anything bad to happen to you."

"I'd rather nothing bad happen to me, too, come to think of it," he smiled. Then he sobered. "If things get hairy, Jake's taking you away. No questions asked. If they want your testimony, they can do it over Teams, Zoom, Google, or what-have-you, too. INTERPOL's not the only organization that needs to realize it's the twenty-first century."

"Oh. Good point," she murmured. "Why are we going in?"

He grunted. "So the trial's not delayed again. That Chalmers bastard is a piece of work, according to Jake. He says there'll be grounds for another extension if you two don't show up in person, and Jake figured you'd rather have it all over with instead of this thing dragging out for years. There's your family to consider, too."

"He could have asked us," she protested.

"No, Officer Alexander's right. We need to get this behind us, for our sake and for our family's sake. No more delays," I said.

"Yeah, Jacey, I was the minority vote. I said to let them extend it until the cows come home, but then Jake pointed out about your family," Billy agreed. "Can't really argue when family's on the line."

Her shoulders slumped. "That's true."

I rubbed her back. "We'll get this all figured out. We'll testify. Masterson will have to let our family go, and we can get on with our lives without this hanging over our heads."

"Makes sense. Sorry, I wasn't thinking about Dad, Jeanie, and the little mite." She looked up at me with misty eyes. "Do you suppose we'll get Will?"

"We'll fight for him," I promised.

"Chalmers said the strangest thing. He called me Will's surrogate, not his mother," she said, frowning.

"Chalmers is an ass, and he was just trying to get a rise out of you, like he did out of me. Because I'm an idiot," I told her.

Jacey gave me a watery smile. "But you're my idiot."

"Good." I kissed some sauce off the corner of her mouth.

"You two are adorable," Billy sighed. "Wish I'd found a wife."

I raised an eyebrow at him. "Billy, you're, like, fifty. You've got time."

"I suppose that's true." He grinned at us. "But how can I fill up this place with kids when you're going to be popping out a dozen or so?"

Her jaw dropped. "I will NOT be popping out a dozen or so!"

"Half a dozen?" I teased.

Jacey scowled at me. "Three at the very most."

"Sold!" I gave her a soft kiss.

She sighed against my lips and this time put her hand innocently on my thigh. I could tell right away she hadn't meant to do it, but it made my pants tight just the same. Dinner couldn't end soon enough!

"I think, after dinner, I'll need to watch a loud action movie," Billy chuckled.

"Good plan," I replied.

Jacey turned pink again and quickly removed her hand. "I just want to be respectful of your space, Billy. It's not like when we were on the road."

"Ah, the road," I reminisced, remembering all ten thousand lakes. I also remembered Jacey going outside her usual comfort zone and getting a bit naughty with Hansen and Bea around.

This place didn't have quite the same vibe. This was Billy's home. Neither of us wanted to make him feel uncomfortable in it.

She swatted me right out of my reverie. "Stop having dirty thoughts around Billy."

"I'm not having dirty thoughts!" I lied.

"Uh-huh. And the Pope is Lutheran," he chuckled. "Okay, you two had better finish eating a little bit. Something tells me you're going to need your strength."

"Billy!" she gasped.

"Just telling it like it is, as the kids say," he laughed.

"You're only fifty, remember?" I reminded him again.

"I'm mature for my age." He grinned.

Jacey just shook her head. She did, however, start eating faster, glancing at me from the corner of her eye.

I was completely on board with the finishing-food-and-going-to-the-bedroom idea she was telegraphing to me. I dug in myself, trying not to get more spaghetti sauce on my shirt than she already had. But it was a losing battle, especially with the speed at which I was eating.

Billy just chuckled to himself and kept eating at a leisurely pace.

When she was finished, I decided I was, too. I picked up our plates, though mine still had a little swatch of salad, and took them to the sink.

"Waste not, want not, Caleb!" he called, still chuckling around a mouthful of garlic bread.

I grimaced but set Jacey's plate in the sink and leaned back around the counter with mine poised at my chest. I wolfed down my salad, then put my plate in the sink as well.

"Suppose someone should do the dishes," he said with a little whistle.

"You're cruel, Billy. Cruel," I groaned, starting to fill the sink with suds.

"And put the food away," he continued with a mischievous smile.

"Cruel," I repeated.

Jacey was already up, picking up the different pots, plates, bowls, and dressings.

"I didn't say I was finished!" Billy protested.

"You're finished, unless you want to do the clean-up," she said in a no-nonsense tone.

He grumbled good-naturedly. "I suppose I'll be taking my dessert in the TV room, then."

"We didn't make dessert," I said flatly. "So you're on your own."

"Talk about cruel!" Billy shook his head. "All right. I *suppose* I can take a pint of Cherries Garcia out of the freezer."

"And wash your spoon," she said to him.

He pouted. "You're both so mean!" He hip-checked me out of the way of the fridge in the small kitchen and got himself a pint of ice cream. Then he grabbed a spoon and wandered off to the TV room.

I grabbed Jacey as soon as she walked into the kitchen with the salad dressings and pinned her against the counter, my lips crashing down on hers.

She dropped the dressings down onto the counter behind her and wrapped her arms around my neck, pressing her body against mine.

I wasn't the only one whose body had changed. She was a bit more muscular herself. It was hot as hell.

"Caleb, we can't do it in here!" she gasped between deep kisses. "We have to finish the dishes—!"

"Fuck the dishes. They can wait. We'll just say we were letting them soak," I growled, nipping her lower lip.

"All night?!" Jacey objected.

I gave her my sexiest smile. "I'm glad we're on the same page about how long we're going to be making love."

She blushed. "Well, I just know when you get started..."

"When *we* get started," I corrected her.

"When *we* get started, we tend not to stop," she mumbled against my lips.

"Then it's time we get started," I whispered in her ear before lifting her in my arms and heading for the bedroom.

LONGER THAN FOREVER

-Jacey-

Caleb's strong arms really were quite sexy. I mean, not that he wasn't ripped before, but now he was super ripped.

He carried me down the hall to our bedroom as though I weighed nothing. I turned the knob and he bumped it shut behind us. He laid me down on the quilt-covered bed, blue and cottagey, then took off his shirt.

"Would you like a nice, close-up view of all the muscles?" he asked, grinning at me.

I swallowed, my throat suddenly dry. "Yes, please."

Caleb tossed his shirt on the nearby window seat, taking the opportunity to twitch the curtains closed just a little bit more. His jeans dipped low on his hips, and I could see he had those muscles that went from hip to groin now. Not that he hadn't *had* them. I was sure they were there under his skin before. But now they were very defined. Just like his abs and pecs had become more defined. And his arms now looked as though he could bench press me. For a while.

But also, with his back turned, I could see the knife scars on his back, and my throat closed. I shuffled across the bed, got up on my knees, and hugged him from behind, kissing a couple of the scars.

"Hey, baby. I'm okay," he murmured, turning in my arms. "More than okay. You're here. We're together. That's all that matters." He gave me a mischievous smile. "Now, I know you've been able to get some sneaky peeks at me with my shirt off, but I can't say the same about you. Let's see those guns!"

I laughed and complied, whipping my shirt up over my head. I was wearing a sports bra—it just made sense for all the farm work we did—but my arms were bare and strong, and I could tell my own chest was a little more defined. I was still a bit curvy, but I'd come to accept that as just me. Caleb liked me that way, and I liked me that way. I didn't see any need to lose the boobs and butt.

"Yummy." He smoothed his hands over my arms. "There's my strong girl." He leaned me back on the bed and unzipped my pants. "Bra. Off."

"Yes, Caleb." I peeled the sports bra off while he slid his hand into my panties. "Pants off?"

"In a minute." He clearly wasn't going to be hurried, even though he'd been tenting his pants at dinner. He cupped my sex with his hand and rubbed my clit with the heel of his hand. "God, it's been too long."

"Longer than forever," I agreed, my hips bucking.

His fingers slid up inside me, two of them, and I moaned and winced at the same time.

"Too long," I explained as my disused passage clamped around his fingers.

Caleb licked his lips. "We're just going to have to do something about that, then." He pulled his hand away and tugged my jeans and panties off.

I lifted my legs to be helpful.

He tugged me to the edge of the bed, then knelt on the floor, tossing my legs over his shoulders.

"Oh God, Caleb," I breathed, fire spreading through my body, and he hadn't even put his mouth on me yet!

"Mhm. You just lay back and enjoy, baby. I've got you." He kissed my mound, then licked his tongue up my seam.

I bucked and gripped the sheets, my thighs squeezing him closer.

He chuckled against me. "Careful, Wonder Woman. You're a lot stronger than you used to be. You might just squash my head!"

With a blush, I eased up, and he entered me with his tongue.

Everything in me focused on that one point. He edged me along, working me with his tongue, then again with his fingers while he sucked my clit.

When I came, I wasn't expecting it. Maybe it was lack of practice, or maybe it was just the magic he was creating between my legs, but fireworks went off all over my body and I moaned loudly, my hands going from the sheets to grip Caleb's hair and hold his magic tongue just where it was.

He slurped loudly, but I still heard his zipper.

"Take me," I begged, letting his hair slip through my fingers as I let him go. "Please, Caleb. Please."

"Crawl up the bed a little bit," he said, pushing his pants and boxers down as he stood up. "Spread your legs wider."

I did as he asked and was rewarded when he got on the bed, hiked one of my knees over his hip, and started to push inside me.

It had been a while, and it wasn't as easy as I'd expected.

"Jesus..." he groaned, "baby, you're really tight. I mean, you're wet, but it's still... it feels good... but does it hurt?"

"A little," I admitted. I put my hands on his muscular shoulders. "Just go slow."

Caleb inched his way in. "Breathe for me, baby."

I hadn't realized I was holding my breath until that moment. I took several deep, bracing breaths as he finished pushing into me. My muscles clamped around him, and he shivered.

"Baby, I'm trying to be really gentle, but it's really hard," he groaned.

"I know it's hard," I tried to joke. "It's inside me. I can tell."

He groaned again and pulled his hips back. My walls clung to his cock as though afraid he wouldn't push it back in.

But he did, and I made a noise I didn't know I was capable of. Something between a whimper and a moan.

"I hear you, baby. We'll get you all loose tonight," he promised, pulling back slowly and thrusting again.

I dug my nails into his skin, my body still on the knife's edge of uncertainty as he kept going. Then, gradually, my muscles began to relax.

"There we go," he sighed and started going a little harder and faster.

"Your patience is appreciated," I gasped, clinging to him as pleasure began to build again.

"I didn't know your vagina had a customer service line," he panted.

I laughed, then came, then burst into heart-wrenching tears.

"Oh, baby, it's okay. I missed this, too," he whispered as his seed spurted into me. He wrapped his arms around me, cupping my ass so he wouldn't slip out, and rolled onto his back. "It's okay. You cry it out."

"It's just… so… everything," I tried to explain my feelings.

"Yeah. It is just so everything," he agreed.

I drew little circles on his chest with my fingertips as I lay on him. "You know I want to return the favor, right?"

"Hmm?" he asked.

"I want to… uh… blow you," I whispered, my cheeks flushing even though I must have blown this man a million times by now.

Caleb didn't make fun of me, though. He just gave me a soft smile and ran his fingers through my hair. "That sounds like the greatest idea in the world. Except I'd have to pull out, and I don't want to."

"You don't want to? Not even for a blowjob?" I asked.

"Not even for a blowjob," he confirmed. He nuzzled me. "I don't mean to sound sappy, but I don't want to lose the connection."

My heart fluttered. "You can be as sappy as you want."

"All right, then. I love you. I love you, and I want to be with you forever," he said.

I sighed happily and snuggled into him. "Longer than forever."

"Longer than forever," he agreed.

BEARING WITNESS

-Caleb-

We white-knuckled it in the back of Officer Alexander's car, me laying across the floor, Jacey laying across the back seat. He'd suggested we go in separate cars, but we'd refused. If someone was being kidnapped or killed this time, we were going together.

This time, Officer Alexander was driving an unmarked vehicle. He said it was fitted with lights and sirens if we needed to make a mad dash for it, but unlike most 'unmarked' police vehicles, this one wasn't obvious at all.

He pulled right up to the front of the courthouse and made a call. "They're here. Yeah. I'll be going with them, but back-up is appreciated. I also need someone to park the car. Thanks." He hung up and looked back at us. "Stay down, just in case there're snipers or something, until we can get the rest of your guards out here."

"Snipers," I muttered. "Great."

"Sounds like something Masterson might do if he was desperate," Jacey mused. "But he likes to make things up close and personal."

"Tell me about it." I shifted on the floor, trying to find a more comfortable position.

"If you two weren't at it all last night, you might not be so uncomfortable," Officer Alexander said, and I couldn't tell if he was being fake stern or actually pissed off.

I grunted. "It's not going to affect our testimony. All we have to do is tell the truth."

Officer Alexander let out a short bark of laughter, and I realized he was messing with us. "Billy said he had to watch the entire Die Hard series—well, the good ones, at least—before he felt safe to go up to bed."

"It had been a while," I groused while Jacey turned pink. "Besides, we weren't that loud."

"Were we?" she squeaked.

He chuckled. "No, you were fine, as far as I know. We just like to give you a hard time."

I wasn't touching that one with a ten-foot pole. "So, these other guards…"

The back door opened, and my feet fell out of the car.

"Are here," Officer Alexander said with a frown. "I don't remember saying you should open the door, sir."

"Well, it's open now," the suited man whose whole demeanor screamed FBI agent replied rudely. "Just be glad we're letting you tag along."

"Letting him tag along?" I scowled. "Look, this guy's kept us safer than most of your agents. In fact, the majority of the agents we encountered could be bought. Are you one of those agents, or did you just wake up on the wrong side of the bed?"

He stared at me as though I was a centipede who'd invaded his space. "I'm sorry, what did your smart mouth just say?"

It looked as though he was planning to put his boot down. I opened my mouth to tell him where he could shove his attitude.

"Let's just go, Caleb. You and I can tell him to stuff it later," Officer Alexander said. "Right now, we need to get you into the courthouse where it's… probably safe."

I sighed but swallowed my pride and sat up. So did Jacey.

"I want you to know," she said primly to the FBI asshole, "Office Alexander is not just here as some courtesy. He's the only reason we're here at all. And if you don't stop being a jerk, we're going to let him take us right back where we came from."

"I'm afraid you're in FBI custody now," the agent sniffed. "So you and your little boyfriend can—"

"Officer Alexander, I want to go home. He can say 'hi' to the Attorney General for us and explain why we're not there," Jacey said.

I reached out to pull the door shut.

The FBI agent wedged his body in the doorway. "You're not running off on us again."

"You're not getting us almost killed again." I gave the door a yank with my newfound farming muscles, which made the man wince at least, but he still kept himself in the doorway.

"You don't seem to understand. Jacey said to take them back. I'll put my foot down on the gas and drag you behind this car if I have to," Officer Alexander warned.

The FBI agent's jaw worked. "Fine. I'll be more warm and cuddly. Now, will you please get out of the car?"

I looked at Jacey, then at Officer Alexander, who nodded. "Okay," I said.

The agent stood out of the way while I wiggled out in the most dignified way I possibly could. Which wasn't very dignified at all. Then I turned and held out my hand to Jacey.

She took my hand, and I pulled her out as well.

Six agents surrounded us immediately, a seventh switching with Officer Alexander and driving the unmarked car away.

Officer Alexander muscled his way into the phalanx to stand next to us. "Keep your heads down."

We both ducked.

Together, the whole group of us shuffled into the courthouse. We stayed huddled until we were through the doors.

Then, Jacey and I went through the metal detectors while the FBI and Officer Alexander went around. The rude FBI agent gave the nod for Officer Alexander to skip the metal detectors.

The Attorney General was waiting for us on the other side. "Caleb,

Jacey," she said, not looking particularly happy to see us. "You've been dodging my calls."

"We didn't even know we had any calls," I said with a frown.

Officer Alexander cleared his throat. "Like I kept telling your office, they weren't going to be made available to be shot at for any kind of redo deposition when you're the one who fucked up."

She stared at him. "Excuse me?"

"You want to hear it in Spanish?" he asked.

"I've had just about enough of you." She took a bracing breath. "As it is, Jacey might be excluded as a witness, and you're on thin ice, Caleb. They're taking this statutory rape and coercion thing very seriously."

"She was eighteen!" I shouted, just as Chalmers walked by with Masterson and their entourage.

Masterson smirked at me, and Chalmers's smile was just as smarmy. "Good to see you, Caleb. I heard you've been having a rough time of it."

"Keep walking. These are protected witnesses, and I will have you arrested for witness tampering, Mr. Masterson," the Attorney General snapped.

"No you won't. You don't want another continuance. All that time to tack on more charges, have my attorneys refute them..." Masterson said.

Margie glowered at him then herded us away. "I can't stand that man."

"All the more reason to put him in jail," I said.

"Hear, hear," Officer Alexander agreed.

"Anyway," she continued, "as I was saying, the judge wants to see you both in chambers. Which means I'll be there, and so will Chalmers. And it doesn't exactly make me look good when I have to tell the judge I can't produce my own witnesses when he calls them."

"You do remember I wheeled that one's ass out of the hospital after all your staff, and the hospital staff, chose money over protecting his life, right?" Officer Alexander said. "He wasn't safe in a *hospital.*"

"Or jail," Jacey added. "Let's not forget jail, you know, where the place is supposed to be crawling with guards?"

She turned bright red. "Yes, well… yes. Let's just go, shall we? Judge Powell is waiting."

With a shrug, I followed her, and Jacey trotted up beside me to hold my hand. Officer Alexander stood beside her so we were flanking her on both sides, and the rest of our retinue fanned out behind.

"I'll be right out here," Officer Alexander said once we arrived at an office door that read 'Judge George Powell.' "Nobody's getting past me."

"Except me," Chalmers chuckled, pushing through the FBI agents to join us. "This is going to be fun." He rubbed his hands together.

I wondered what was making him so confident until the door swung open and there sat Hank and my mother, holding our half-brother.

"Jacey! Caleb! Thank God you're all right!" my mother fretted, crossing the room to give us both a hug.

Hank, much to my surprise, stood shakily from his wheelchair. Leaning heavily on a cane, he started over to Jacey.

I gently set my mother aside and put myself between him and my girl. "I don't think so, Hank."

"Look, I'm not gonna hit her. I just want to see that she's okay," he said, exasperated.

"You're not going to hit her *this* time. As I'm sure Judge Powell is aware, a basic canvass did yield nine people willing to swear under oath that you attacked your daughter on the street," the Attorney General inserted coldly. She turned to Judge Powell, an older, yet distinguished-looking, gentleman sitting behind his desk. "In fact, Your Honor, I don't even know what we're doing here, given if there was any coercion going on, it was clearly Mr. Collins and not Mr. Killeen. Mr. Collins is the only one who has threatened violence of any kind in this room."

"He locked me in my room and wouldn't let me out," Jacey told the judge quietly. "I was eighteen."

"You still are for another week, I believe," the judge said. He looked at my mother. "And I thought you said your husband did not trap your stepdaughter in your home. That she, in fact, assaulted you, under your son's influence."

"*What?!*" I yelled. I glared at my mother, who at least had the decency to look at the floor. "I was kicked out of the house when she 'assaulted' you, and the way Jacey tells it, she pushed you out of the way because *you* were blocking the door!"

My mother hugged our brother against her like a shield. "Well, I was pregnant. She could have really hurt me."

"That's not what we discussed, darling," Hank said quickly. "Remember? I remember she slammed you into a wall."

"Are you going to swear to that under oath, Mrs. Collins?" the judge asked, arching an eyebrow at her.

My mother paled.

"Jeanie, just tell the man the truth," Hank pressed.

She burst into tears. "It's the way Caleb said. I didn't want to lie, Your Honor. I just don't want to be stuck with Masterson forever, and he said..."

"Your Honor, I think I need a moment to talk with my witnesses," Chalmers interrupted.

"And I think you need to sit down, Mr. Chalmers," the judge said evenly.

It was Chalmers's turn to go white. It made a dark place in me very happy to see his hand shake as he squirmed into a seat.

"Mr. Killeen. Ms. Collins. Please also be seated. Ms. Jepsen, I'm now even more interested to know why we couldn't have cleared this problem up weeks ago," Judge Powell grumped.

"Your Honor, I apologize..." the Attorney General began.

"Masterson tried to kill me, sir, in jail and in the hospital. Only, in the hospital, he tried to do it himself," I said. "So our good friend Officer Alexander of the state police has been keeping us safe in an undisclosed location. Nowhere was safe, sir. Our FBI handlers have been killed more than once. Others have been corrupted into trying to kill us. I count ourselves lucky to have had someone like Office

Alexander on our side, fielding requests. I know it might not sound like a good reason to you, Your Honor, but I'm just about damn near done wandering with a target on my back. And on Jacey's back. So we're coming out just this one last time. That's it."

"Slander!" Chalmers shouted. "That is all slander!"

"Shut up, Chalmers." The judge grunted. He frowned at me. "So, you're giving me an ultimatum? After both of your deposition disasters, if I want to hear testimony, you're only willing to give it today?"

I swallowed hard then nodded firmly. "We're not doing this again, sir."

Judge Powell sat back in his chair. "Then I suppose we have no choice." He glared at Chalmers. "You can take your coercion and statutory rape charges against the protected witness and shove them up your ass, Chalmers. You'll be very, very lucky if, by the end of the day, you *and* your client aren't facing witness tampering charges. Do you understand?"

Chalmers puffed up, then deflated when the judge was unmoved by his swagger. "Yes, Your Honor."

"As for the trial, well, we'd better get to it. Seems there's a time limit on how long I have these witnesses," the judge said. "And I would like the FBI to now take custody of Hank and Jeanie Collins and put them... well, jail doesn't seem safe these days, nor does Witness Protection. Keep them out in the hall until this is over, and we'll all figure something out."

"Yes, Your Honor," the Attorney General replied. She opened the office door and gave instructions to the FBI.

"One of these days, Caleb, you're going to pay for what you've done to my little girl." Hank growled as he collapsed back into his chair and was wheeled past me.

"I promise you, Hank, I feel exactly the same way," I shot back.

"Children, please. Try to keep it out of court. What I want from you today is your testimony about William Masterson Sr.," Judge Powell scolded us. "Well, Mr. Killeen's. Not yours. You should thank your lucky stars you didn't lie under oath today, Mr. Collins."

Hank bristled, but before he could say anything else, the Attorney

General nodded to the FBI agent who was wheeling him, and Hank was taken out into the hall.

"The Attorney General will show you where to sit until you're called," Judge Powell said to Jacey and me. "I'm afraid you won't be allowed into the courtroom until that time."

"Yes, Your Honor," I responded.

The Attorney General shooed us out.

BLOW THE MAN DOWN

-Jacey-

I sat in a little side room with Caleb and Officer Alexander, the stuffy FBI agent and a few others stationed outside the door. Caleb winced at some bad coffee—I hadn't even bothered to try it—but Officer Alexander seemed to be enjoying it. Hours ticked by on an overhead round-faced clock. I wondered what was going on in the courtroom.

Then there was a knock on the door. "Jocelyn Collins, you're up," the stuffy FBI agent said.

"Me? First?" I gaped, surprised.

"You, yeah. Let's go," he replied with a huff.

Caleb squeezed my hand. "You're going to do great."

I gave him a weak smile. "Thanks. I hope so."

"Give the bastard what for," Officer Alexander said. "And by that, of course, I mean just tell the truth. And don't let that Chalmers asshole rile you up."

"I'll do my best," I responded. My feet felt heavy as I walked with the FBI agent through the double doors of the courtroom then into court itself.

Facing Judge Powell, who looked very intimidating in his robe, I could see the Attorney General and a handful of her staff to his left, with Chalmers, Masterson, and their army to his right. The row behind Chalmers and Masterson was filled with corporate-looking types, and I decided they must be his lawyers as well. They'd come out in force.

They all looked at me like wolves standing over a steak.

I gulped.

"Ms. Collins. Please take the stand," Judge Powell said, gesturing to the somewhat lower spot next to him.

Taking a deep breath, I forced my feet forward and went up to the witness box. A bailiff came over and held out a Bible.

"Place your left hand on the Bible," he instructed.

I did.

"Do you swear to tell the truth, the whole truth, and nothing but the truth, so help you God?" he intoned.

I plucked up all my courage and nodded. "I do swear."

"Good," Judge Powell said. "Go ahead and take a seat, Ms. Collins."

Tucking my skirt behind my knees, I sat.

"You may begin, Ms. Jepsen," the judge encouraged.

The Attorney General stood and walked up to stand between me and her table of staff. "Ms. Collins," she began, giving me a steadying look that took away some of my nerves, "will you please detail, for the court, the circumstances that led you to come into contact with Mr. William Masterson Sr. and his business dealings?"

There was no jury, so I figured Masterson must have wanted a verdict straight from the bench. Maybe he'd be afraid they'd all hate him after Caleb's and my testimony. He wasn't wriggling his way out because of me, though.

I looked up at the judge. "Uh, sir? This could take a while. Is that okay? There's a lot to cover."

"You go right ahead. I may ask clarifying questions, and so may Ms. Jepsen. If you hear Mr. Chalmers object, or if I stop you, you need to stop right away, though."

"Okay." I nervously gripped the arms of the chair then began at the beginning. "We were going camping for my birthday in Uppsala

—that's a part of Ontario, Canada—at this lake we go to all the time..."

"Shimmer Lake?" the Attorney General asked.

"Yes, ma'am. We go every year. Well, my dad and I went every year. That year, about a year ago now, my dad wanted Jeanie, his new wife, and her son, Caleb, to come, too. Caleb and I weren't on good terms then exactly. I sort of blurted out that I liked him at my fifteenth birthday...." I blushed. "And he basically stayed away after that at college. But somehow we all ended up going. A couple of days in, at camp, my dad said something—I don't even remember what anymore—and it really pissed Caleb off, and me, too, so we took off in a boat together...."

The judge nodded along as I told our story, from getting marooned to running into the murderous owner of the cabin we'd taken refuge in, to running into Masterson's loggers.

"Only, we didn't know they were his loggers yet. The man in charge just told us it was an illegal logging operation. They were going to kill us, but then, they didn't," I said.

"There's gratitude for you," Chalmers muttered.

"Mr. Chalmers, must I remind you every time I see you that I don't mind holding you in contempt of court?" Judge Powell sighed.

"I'll pay the fine," Chalmers snorted.

Judge Powell's eyes narrowed on him. "You don't even know what it'll be yet. This time."

Chalmers waved a hand. "Fine. Please continue, Ms. Collins. Your story is riveting."

"Well, now that we have your permission," the Attorney General said with false sweetness. She shook her head and turned back to me. "When did you learn the logging operation belonged to Mr. Masterson?"

"When Will brought us to his house," I replied, sadness washing over me as I remembered Masterson's son. "He died."

"That's a bit of an understatement, isn't it, Ms. Collins?" the Attorney General said sympathetically. "He was a friend?"

I nodded. "A friend of Caleb's, but later also a friend of mine."

"What happened to William Masterson Jr.?" the Attorney General asked.

"He committed suicide," I whispered. "His father... the whole situation..."

"Objection. She can't know what poor Will Jr. was thinking when he killed himself," Chalmers said.

"Sustained. Ms. Jepsen, let's contain the line of questioning to Mr. Masterson's crimes, if we can," Judge Powell reprimanded her lightly.

I couldn't think of a worse crime than causing your son to kill himself and then turning his funeral into some sort of farce by acting sad at it when you'd called your own son weak for refusing to be a part of your bad deeds anymore, but I supposed it wasn't possible for me to tell that all secondhand. Masterson had enough other reprehensible crimes to hold him forever, anyway. At least, I hoped they'd hold him forever.

"Ms. Collins, did you have a child with Will Jr.?" the Attorney General asked.

I chewed my lip. "Yes, but he was born through invitro."

"Objection. Facts not in evidence," Chalmers said.

The Attorney General rolled her eyes. "Your Honor, I have the Mastersons' private doctor willing to swear, under oath, that he delivered Will III and that Ms. Collins had him, so I don't see where —"

"The fertility doctor will have a different story, Your Honor," Chalmers interrupted.

Judge Powell all but growled. "Approach."

The Attorney General and Chalmers both went to the judge. "Are you suggesting the witness is committing perjury, Mr. Chalmers?" the judge asked.

"Not at all, Your Honor," Chalmers said. "She couldn't possibly know. I mean, she was the child's surrogate. But she's not his mother."

"Come again?" the Attorney General asked before I almost did.

"The fertility doctor used donor eggs. A simple DNA test will prove it," Chalmers replied smugly. "And Ms. Collins was paid for her services..."

"I don't understand," I blurted, my heart seizing. "Masterson told me Will was mine."

"I'm sure it was just a misunderstanding between Masterson and a hormonal young woman," Chalmers simpered.

I was going to kill him. I looked at Masterson, who also looked smug. I was going to kill them both. "You're telling me I'm *not* Will's biological mother?!"

"No, dearie. You're not," Chalmers said.

Tears stung my eyes. I wiped them away with my sleeve. Judge Powell handed me a box of tissues, and I had to keep dabbing because the tears wouldn't stop. "I don't care," I croaked. "He's my son, and I want him."

"You see how delusional she is, Your Honor?" Chalmers observed sadly. "Paid to be a surrogate and now under some misapprehension that his grandfather is some kind of evil international villain..."

"His grandfather *is* an evil, international villain! He drugged me! He kidnapped me! He watched me have sex with my boyfriend! Oh God..." I moaned, dropping my head into my hands.

"I think Ms. Collins needs a minute, Margerie," the judge said softly. "Why don't you bring her out into the hall. You can't put her back in with Mr. Killeen, though, until he's given his testimony. I'm sure you realize that."

She glared at Chalmers, a glare so dark it sucked light from the room. "You have absolutely no soul, Rob."

"None whatsoever," he replied cheerfully.

"I'm going to have you disbarred someday," she continued.

"I'd like to see you try," he said.

"Children," Judge Powell sighed. "That's enough. Ms. Collins, I'm very sorry, but you're going to be taken to another room for a little while. Since we don't have a lot of time with them today, Ms. Jepsen, I suggest, in the meantime, we hear from Mr. Killeen."

"Yes, Your Honor," she said and offered me her hand to help me out of the witness box.

I raised the Kleenex box back up to the judge, but he shook his head. "You take that with you."

"Thank you, sir," I whispered, then followed the Attorney General out.

The bailiff followed us and then turned in the direction of the room I'd come from, no doubt going to get Caleb. The FBI agents outside that room saw the Attorney General leading me to another and a few peeled off to guard that door.

I sat down, shaking, inside a cold, empty room. I wanted Caleb so badly. I wanted him to hug me and tell me everything was going to be okay.

"We can try to get custody of Will," the Attorney General said kindly as I sat there, feeling my world crumble.

When I looked up, I could tell she was *just* being kind. "There's really no hope, is there?"

She winced. "I… well… with you not being his biological mother, and you basically being in Witness Protection… it will be a very hard sell. But that doesn't mean you don't deserve the best lawyer and the best possible shot at it."

"Against Masterson's army," I replied hopelessly. "Giving him another opportunity to take a shot at us when we come out of hiding for the trial."

"There is that," she said. "I… I really am sorry. I didn't have any contact with this fertility doctor, or I wouldn't have let them blindside you like that. You can be sure I'll be lodging a complaint as well as objecting in court."

"I should have known Masterson would have a trick up his sleeve to rattle me," I murmured. The tears coursed down my cheeks again. "Please, can you go question Caleb? I want him here as soon as possible."

She nodded. "I can do that."

"Thank you." I covered my face with my hands as she left.

What were we going to do?

THE OTHER SHOE DROPS

-Caleb-

When Jacey didn't return, but the rude FBI agent stuck his head in and called for me, I was beyond worried. *Why isn't she here? Where did she go?*

"Put some hustle in it," he complained. "It's your turn to testify."

I scowled at him but stood just the same. "Officer Alexander? Could you go check and see how Jacey is doing? I have a bad feeling."

"You know, by now, you two should be calling me Jake, right?" he replied with a grimace.

"I'll take it under advisement," I said.

"I'll go check on her," Jake assured me. "You go testify."

I nodded and stepped out of the room, following the bailiff into the courtroom.

The Attorney General was already there. She looked frazzled but determined. I was counting on her determination.

"Please be seated, Mr. Killeen," Judge Powell said. He glared at Chalmers. "And no more shenanigans from you."

I wondered what 'shenanigans' he'd pulled on Jacey, but I didn't have time to contemplate it long because the bailiff came back over with a Bible and swore me in.

"Mr. Killeen, how did you come to know about Mr. Masterson Sr.'s various business dealings?" the Attorney General started off, straightening her jacket as she stood.

Jacey had answered the same way I was about to, I was certain, so I simply launched into it. "Jacey's—Jocelyn Collins, that is—her father is an asshat…"

"Please try to keep the language clean, Mr. Killeen," Judge Powell interrupted, but not unkindly.

"Sorry. He's… um… difficult, to say the least. He shot off his mouth about Jacey, and we got into it. I mean, it probably would have come to blows if I hadn't taken the boat. Jacey came with me. We were in Canada on a fishing trip. Anyway, took the boat, got lost, got stranded. Found this nice cabin with food and supplies, but it turned out it belonged to this complete psychopath. We had to escape him. When we did, we ran into these loggers, and we thought they'd help us, but it turned out to be an illegal logging operation. We found out later it was one of Masterson's businesses," I said.

"And how did you find out later?" the Attorney General asked. "When?"

I took a deep breath and went into detail, talking about Hank discovering us and Will offering us refuge in his home. Everything from being guests to being prisoners to being unwilling accomplices.

"And can you identify the man who did all these things? Is he in court today?" the Attorney General continued.

I looked Masterson right in the eye as I stabbed a finger in his direction. "William Masterson Sr. He's right there."

"Thank you, Mr. Killeen," the Attorney General said and returned to her table.

Chalmers, the bastard, then got up and offered the courtroom a saccharine sweet smile. "Caleb—may I call you Caleb?"

"No," I replied.

He chuckled. "Feisty. Hostile?"

"Objection. You can't treat him as a hostile witness just because he doesn't like you," the Attorney General groused. "He hasn't refused to answer any of your questions."

"Sustained. Mr. Chalmers, if you don't mind, could you get to your questions?" Judge Powell asked with long-suffering patience.

"Of course, Your Honor. Just testing the waters," he smiled. He turned back to me. "What happened to the 'complete psychopath'?"

My jaw worked. "I hit him with a rock when he was going to attack Jacey."

"And what was the result of that?" Chalmers asked.

"He died," I said in a clipped tone.

Chalmers raised an eyebrow at me. "He died? Does that mean you murdered him?"

"Objection. Facts not in evidence," the Attorney General said, standing.

"Sustained. Tread carefully, Mr. Chalmers," Judge Powell warned.

"Your Honor, the witness just admitted to murder," Chalmers protested.

"What I heard him admit to was defense of another," the Attorney General argued. "If not self-defense."

"He did shoot me," I said.

Chalmers snorted. "I guess we only have your word on that."

I scowled at him then smoothed back some of my hair to reveal the graze mark near my temple.

That shut him up. Actually, it had his mouth hanging open like a landed fish.

"Bailiff, I would like you to take photographs of the new evidence for both parties," the judge said, looking at my scar.

"Th-That's right! That's new evidence! It was not put forth in discovery," Chalmers spluttered.

"Nobody asked," I responded as the bailiff came over with his phone to take pictures.

"Still, I had no chance to review the evidence before trial. I'm asking for a continuance…" Chalmers said.

Judge Powell's eyes narrowed. "Denied."

"I'm noting my objection to that in court records," Chalmers advised him.

"You do that," Judge Powell replied. "My decision stands. Do you have any more questions, Mr. Chalmers?"

Chalmers puffed out his chest. "Many, Your Honor."

"Then, by all means, continue," the judge said.

Chalmers took a deep breath then got his swagger back. He came right up to the witness box and leaned on the ledge. "Mr. Killeen. You've killed more than once, haven't you?"

"It's been an interesting year," I replied.

"I take it that means 'yes'?" Chalmers asked.

"Yes," I said tersely.

"Then I suppose you're asking us to believe the testimony of a murderer," Chalmers snorted. He shook his head at the judge. "I just don't see how we can do that, Your Honor."

The Attorney General gave a long sigh. "Your Honor," she said. "Do you want me to go through every single one of Mr. Killeen's crimes to have him tell you, every time, he was under duress, or can we just ask him once and move on?"

Judge Powell pursed his lips. "I'm afraid we'll have to go through them one at a time. Otherwise, Mr. Killeen may be discredited, and I will have to disregard his testimony."

With a soft groan, the Attorney General looked at her colleague to her right. He opened his briefcase and pulled out a large accordion file bursting at the gills with papers.

I decided that had to be the 'Caleb Killeen Misdeeds' file.

This could take weeks!

WE BROKE FOR LUNCH, but I still wasn't able to go see Jacey. I wolfed down a turkey wrap then waited impatiently to be called again. Jake was nowhere to be seen. They were probably keeping him from me as well, now that he knew what they'd blindsided Jacey with. I had a strong feeling she was chased right off the stand. Her testimony hadn't lasted nearly long enough.

I got up and paced the room as the rude FBI agent watched me dispassionately. "I don't suppose you're going to tell me what happened with Jacey?"

"Not a chance," he responded. "But sit tight. They'll be calling you back in there soon."

"I hope so. I want to get this day over with." I grumbled. I was exhausted, and we'd only covered half the folder the other attorney had pulled out of his briefcase.

"You're probably not going to finish today, but we'll put you up in a nice hotel," the agent said with a smirk. "Not a whole lot your cop friend is going to be able to do about it, either."

"You'd better get a couple of cots, then, because we're not leaving this building," I told him. "Not with the danger out there. It's going to be bad enough leaving just the once when the trial is over."

He shrugged. "Your call, I guess. Makes my life easier."

"No, it makes you alive, period. The Trinary is after us for the ransom on our heads," I said. "So… you're welcome."

He seemed to be thinking the same thing I was—that Bea and Hansen had been killed by those bastards—and they were excellent agents. Probably a lot more skilled than he was. "I suppose I should thank you," he murmured.

The bailiff knocked on the door. "We're ready for you, Mr. Killeen."

I stopped pacing and strode out of the room, almost racing him to the door of the courtroom.

"I will remind you that you're still under oath," Judge Powell said after I sat down. "And I'm afraid, Mr. Killeen, that we're not going to be able to get through even just your full testimony today."

"That's all right, Your Honor. I've already requested cots from the FBI," I replied, sighing inwardly. At least the man was honest, but this was getting grueling, and I imagined it was only going to get more grueling the next day.

The Attorney General shuffled some papers in front of her. "Your Honor, we've reached an agreement."

Judge Powell blinked. "You did this over lunch?"

"Yes, sir. Mr. Masterson has agreed to plead guilty to all charges against him in return for a twenty-five-year sentence and retaining custody of his grandson. He said he will arrange proper care for William III," the Attorney General said.

I frowned. "Your Honor, respectfully, that's not gonna happen. Jacey and I will be raising Will as our son."

"You're not the father," Chalmers sniffed.

"I will be," I said. "Jacey's his mother, and that's all that matters to me."

"Oh, good. Then you should have no objection," Chalmers grinned.

Judge Powell rubbed his temples. "Not this again. Are you just doing this for fun, Mr. Chalmers?"

"No. But it is fun." Chalmers smirked at me. "Do you know why Ms. Collins went running out of here?"

"Enlighten me," I grunted.

"She just found out that Will *isn't* her son. She was just the surrogate," Chalmers said. "Mr. Masterson Sr. used donor eggs for the invitro fertilization."

I frowned at him. "That can't possibly be true. That bastard told us the whole time that Jacey is Will's mother."

"I have a DNA test that proves it," Chalmers said.

Rage boiled under my skin. "You said this to Jacey while she was on the stand?"

"I did, indeed," Chalmers confirmed.

There were many, many unpleasant things I wanted to do to Chalmers right then. But I wanted to see Jacey more. "I don't care. She doesn't care. We're raising Will. Period. We owe it to his father, if nothing else."

"You're not raising my grandson," Masterson piped up. "He'll grow up as weak as both of you."

"I wouldn't call them weak, Mr. Masterson," the Attorney General said. "Quite the opposite, actually. And this agreement, if you sanction it, Your Honor, will come with the caveat that Will III be given a genetic test administered by a lab the Federal Government approves of."

"Bring me the signed plea documents with the maternity *and* paternity results, and I will render my decision next week." Judge Powell sighed heavily. "You are free to leave with Ms. Collins, Mr. Killeen. If you are needed, you will be recalled."

I shook my head vehemently. "Your Honor, please. You can't let Will be raised by that… that monster!"

"It's out of your hands now, Mr. Killeen. You have no say in the matter," Judge Powell said. "Now, go."

I wanted to argue more, but the bailiff came up beside me, and I could tell he was prepared to remove me by force, if necessary.

Glowering at everyone in the room, but especially Masterson, I stood and left with the bailiff.

BYE, BYE BABY

-Jacey-

When the door swung open, I was in the middle of my sixth sobbing jag. Caleb came straight to my side, kneeling beside my chair and hugging my waist.

"You were gone so long," I whispered, putting my wadded-up Kleenex down so I could hug him back properly. "Why were you gone so long?"

"They wanted to go over all of my crimes so that there was nothing Chalmers could appeal." His voice was muffled against my clothes. "Baby, are you okay?"

It was a stupid question. I was not okay, and we both already knew that. "Will isn't mine. I don't know if we can fight for custody of him," I said, my voice trembling.

He was quiet, and that was a good indicator to me that something else was terribly, terribly wrong. "Caleb?"

"Let me just hug you for a minute," he sighed, squeezing me tighter.

Terribly, *terribly* wrong. "Okay," I reluctantly agreed.

"I'll let you two have the room." I'd forgotten Officer Alexander was even there.

I gave him a watery, but grateful, smile. "Thank you."

He nodded and left.

I stroked Caleb's hair, wondering what the awful news was going to be, becoming more terrified as the minutes stretched on. "Caleb?" I finally said again.

"Masterson made a deal." He rocked back on his knees and took my hands. "He'll take twenty-five years in prison."

"But that's good news," I replied. "That's wonderful news, actually."

He swallowed. "In return… he keeps custody of Will."

My heart stopped. "No."

"That's what I said. They're doing a maternity and paternity test through the government this time to make sure, but Judge Powell is really considering it. He even told me to keep my nose out of it," he said miserably.

"Oh God." The horror in my belly made me sick to my stomach, and I had to push Caleb away so I could get to the garbage can and throw up.

He came over and held back my hair while I emptied what little I'd been able to eat that day into the trash. "I'm going to ask Jake if we can get a lawyer or something and fight this."

I wiped my mouth. "Ask him now," I croaked. "Ask him right now."

"Okay." He rubbed my back for a moment then went to the door and called for Officer Alexander.

I sank to my knees on the floor.

Officer Alexander came in and looked down at me with concern, coming over to help me up, but I waved him off.

"What's going on?" he asked Caleb.

Caleb explained what had happened in the courtroom. "Is there any way we can get a lawyer and fight this?"

Officer Alexander looked pained. "It'd be a hard sell. You'd need a really good lawyer, and you don't have any of your own money."

He was right. We were at the mercy of the very government that was going to put Will beyond our reach. "Oh God," I whispered again.

Caleb's chin jutted out mutinously. "There has to be something we can do. Maybe if this case gets really famous, or we go to the papers, or…"

"You want him to try harder to kill you? Plus, I think this one's getting sealed, and you're both going to have to sign non-disclosure agreements along with the jury. What they've been telling the public is that Masterson is in trouble for insider trading," Officer Alexander said.

"Yeah. Of people," Caleb responded bitterly.

"You know that. I know that. But if you tell the public, you're going to lose what little protection you have." Officer Alexander sounded glum. "I'm so sorry, you two, but I think you're going to have to give this one up."

I struggled to my feet, abandoning the garbage can. Caleb rushed over to help me. "'This one'?" I hissed. "There is no 'this one.' This is my son. I don't care if he's biologically mine or not. I carried him in my body. He's a *baby* in the hands of that… that…"

"Monster," Caleb provided.

"Yes, that monster!" I agreed. "He's innocent. He doesn't deserve to grow up in that asshole's claws!"

"I hear what you're saying," Officer Alexander replied slowly. "And Lord knows I agree with you, but there's nothing we can do, Jacey. Nothing. Do you understand? I want you to tell me you understand before we go back out there. You can't make a scene."

My hands balled into fists. "If they don't want a scene, they shouldn't be trying to take Will away from us."

He moved to block the door. "You can't go out there like this. I need you to sit and think about what you're doing first. Really think about it. If, after an hour, you're still set on doing what I think you're going to do, then I'll let you out, and you can do whatever you want. But I really want you to think about this first."

I stormed toward him, but Caleb caught my arm. "Let's give it an hour, Jacey. We can come up with a good plan of attack."

"A good plan of attack," I echoed. I glowered at Officer Alexander, but what Caleb was saying made sense. It would be best to go in with some sort of plan.

Caleb sat down and pulled me into his lap. He rubbed my back, and my rage began to recede. Slightly. "I love you, baby."

"I love you, too. But don't call me 'baby' right now," I said.

He nodded. "Okay."

For the longest time, we were both silent, the cogs in our heads turning as we thought over the situation.

"We could—" Caleb began uncertainly.

"Maybe—?" I said at the same time.

"You go first," Caleb encouraged me.

"No, you. My idea is stupid," I mumbled.

"Mine, too," Caleb sighed. "Shit."

Officer Alexander just leaned quietly against the door, waiting for us to come to the same conclusion he had half an hour ago.

However, I was not willing to give up. "We could steal him?" I suggested. "Just slip onto the estate and take him."

"With all the cameras?" Caleb reminded me in frustration.

Oh. Right. The cameras. How could I forget?! My desperate mind was now trying to discount reality. "Maybe..."

There was a knock on the door. "Caleb? Jacey? The bailiff needs to come in and get cheek swabs from both of you," the Attorney General said through the door.

I wasn't a huge fan of hers right now and was about to tell her where she could go with her cheek swabs, but then, it occurred to me it wouldn't be beyond Masterson to just torture us this way as long as he could. Maybe I was Will's mother after all. "Okay," I murmured.

Officer Alexander stepped away from the door, and it swung in. The bailiff, wearing vinyl gloves, was carrying two test packets with him.

"I want you to know, even if this test comes back that I'm not the mother, we're fighting for custody of Will," I said to the Attorney General just before the bailiff rubbed a cotton swab against the inside of my cheek.

"That won't be happening, Jacey. I'm sorry." She did sound truly regretful, but it just made my blood boil.

"I don't need you to be sorry. This isn't right! He's just a baby," I argued.

The bailiff finished swabbing Caleb's cheek before he chimed in. "We want Will. It'll be the best environment for him to grow up with us."

"What? Grow up always on the run? Are you sure about that?" she asked.

She might as well have stabbed me in the back. "What?"

"That's the argument I will use against your custody plea, if you can even get a lawyer to sponsor one," she said. "You two don't have a stable environment for a baby."

"Oh, and Masterson does?" Caleb seethed.

"More stable than you, unfortunately," the Attorney General sighed. "Not that we won't be keeping a very close watch. One wrong move, and that child is going into the system. I wrote it into the agreement."

I looked at Caleb. "Foster care?"

"As wholesome as *that* sounds, maybe you just give him to us now, and we call it even," Caleb said. "We've got more than a few complaints about corruption in government agencies."

"Good luck with that. Look, I really am on your side. This plea bargain is a good thing. Twenty-five years isn't a short prison sentence, and maybe in that amount of time, he'll be able to reflect on his actions. Hell, I don't know, maybe he'll find Jesus. What I do know is Masterson can provide for Will like you can't. Education. Resources..."

"Love?" I spat.

The Attorney General winced. "He probably loves Will in his own, twisted way."

"Because that's a healthy growing environment." I shook my head. "You're selling Will's happiness and future to put a man in jail for twenty-five years. That's not okay."

"It has to be okay. I'm thinking of the futures of thousands of children Masterson is taking away by throwing them in a shipping crate and selling them into the worst kind of slavery," she said. "I have to think about the greater good."

"I'll be sure to tell Will that you said that someday," Caleb snorted.

After a long sigh, she said, "I will get the agreement amended to state that, if and when, Masterson screws things up taking care of Will, that Will must be delivered into your care. But that's the best I can do. In return, you need to let this go, and sign non-disclosure agreements."

Caleb looked at me. "That's… actually a pretty good deal."

"What?" I replied, shocked by his agreeing with her.

"Think about it. It won't take more than a month for Masterson to fuck up. Then we get Will free and clear," Caleb said.

I did think about it and decided he was right. "We want to see it in writing first, though," I told the Attorney General cautiously.

"I thought you might." She stepped toward the door. "Give me about an hour and a half. That should give us all time to get things settled. We're rushing your DNA tests as we speak."

"Good," I said.

When she left, Officer Alexander closed the door behind her, and I leaned against Caleb, just watching the minute hand on the clock over the door tick around and around.

"He has to be mine," I whispered. "He just has to be. Masterson is playing an awful joke."

"It doesn't matter either way," Caleb said firmly, stroking my arm. "He's ours. That's final. It doesn't matter what the DNA tests say."

I nodded. He was right. Will was ours either way.

An hour and a half, then two hours passed. I was gripping Caleb's thighs by the time there was another knock at the door.

The Attorney General looked exhausted, and she wouldn't make eye contact with either of us. "The results came back…"

"And?" I asked, my guts knotted with dread.

"Neither one of you is biologically related to Will III. I'm sorry," she said. "But you do have to hold up your end."

My throat closed. My eyes stung with tears. I would have sobbed if I could get one past my restricted airway.

Caleb wrapped his arms around me and held me tightly. "It'll be a month at most," he said to me. "There's no way that man could raise a cactus, much less a child, no matter who he hires."

I tried to catch my breath. The world was spinning. The only things holding me together were Caleb's strong arms. "But... he... we..."

"Just a month at most," he reassured me. "Then he'll be with us, and no one can say boo about it."

Uncertainty coiled in my chest, but I decided Caleb was right. This was the best way forward. It might be the only way forward.

"Where are the non-disclosure agreements?" I finally sighed.

The Attorney General set them in front of us. "You won't regret this," she said.

Her words sounded ominous rather than reassuring. I read the agreement carefully, and so did Caleb, just to make sure we weren't signing away any rights we wanted to keep.

Then, dragging in a deep breath, I initialed, initialed, and signed my name at the bottom.

FALSE HOPE

-Caleb-

A month later, Masterson was in prison, and Jacey and I were back on the farm. She had spoken to me less and less as the weeks passed and was now icing me out altogether. I didn't blame her. I'd given her false hope.

But I'd been so sure Masterson was going to bungle it with Will. A bad nanny. Something. Instead, Will was doing very well, according to the Attorney General. Masterson had even been 'kind' enough to send us photos and videos of Will, playing and happy as a clam. 'Kind' was overstating things a bit. He did it to torture us, especially Jacey.

We had a photo of Will framed by our bedside. I wondered when she was going to pick it up and leave to go sleep in another room. She was so stiff beside me at night. She flinched away when I touched her.

I took my anger and despair out on the stables, mucking for all I was worth.

"I'm taking Jacey into the city today," Billy said, startling me. "I wanted to tell you before we left."

"She asked that I not go along," I inferred, tossing manure with sharp precision into a wheelbarrow.

He sighed. "Yeah, she did ask that."

"It's fine," I said, launching more manure. "If she doesn't want me along, then I won't go along. It's not like we're attached at the hip."

"Yeah. Pull the other one," he snorted. "You two need to fix this, you know? You're both causing each other a lot of pain."

I whirled on him, dropping the shovel on the ground. "She's the one who won't talk to me. Who won't let me touch her. I don't know what to do. I can't magic Will here, and I can't take back what I said at the courthouse. So if she wants to give me the silent treatment, fine. I deserve it." I raked a hand through my hair. "Maybe I should start thinking about having WITSEC place me somewhere else. I'm probably just making her more unhappy by being here."

"Don't give up yet, Caleb. You love each other very much. Give it time," he said.

I took a deep breath. "I'll try. I just don't want to keep hurting her."

"I know. Just give it some more time. It might take a couple of months, but you'll make your way back to each other." He clapped me on a sweaty shoulder.

With a nod, I leaned against a stable door. The horse inside turned his head and started chewing on my hair.

He laughed. "The horses like you fine. Horses and dogs, they always know good people."

"Thanks, Billy. Have fun in the city," I said.

He stepped back out of the stables, and soon, I heard his truck fire up. I didn't go to look or wave. I was pretty sure Jacey didn't want to see me.

I kept doing chores for the rest of the day. There were horses, pigs, and chickens to feed, cows to milk, all kinds of things to keep me busy. I was just finishing up oiling the hinges on the screen door when the truck returned.

Billy, ever the gentleman, hopped out and went around to open Jacey's door. She looked at me, and I flinched, expecting coldness again. But, while there was caution in her gaze, there was also something now that looked like budding... hope?

I wiped my hands off on an old cloth and walked over to the truck. "Hi," I said, equally cautious.

"Hi," she replied shyly. She held out her hand. "I'm Jacey."

Did she get a lobotomy? I took her hand, confused. "Caleb."

"Caleb." The way she said my name made my heart melt. "Can we go to our room and talk?"

I nodded. "I'd like that."

Billy gave me a wink as we mounted the front steps and went into the house. "I'll just finish up with the door here. You kids figure things out."

"Thanks," Jacey said.

The walk to our bedroom seemed to take forever, and at the same time, my nervousness decided it didn't take long enough. I was afraid to hope. I was terrified it might be over, and she was letting me down easy.

I closed the door behind us with a sense of impending doom.

I nearly jumped out of my skin when Jacey put a hand on my naked back. "Baby?" I asked, turning around.

"Yes. That's what I wanted to talk about, but right now…" she wrapped her arms around my waist and pressed her cheek against my chest. "I missed you."

I should have been overjoyed. On some level, I was ecstatic. But anger bubbled up in me as well, and I gripped her upper arms and pushed her just far enough away that I could look her in the eyes. "Jacey, you've been icing me out for almost a month."

Her eyes welled with tears, but she quickly dashed them away. "I know. I'm sorry. I shouldn't have blamed you. That wasn't fair. And I even knew it wasn't fair while I was doing it. I'm so stupid…."

"You're not stupid. I'm stupid. I really thought Masterson would botch the whole thing. But he didn't. Us signing Will's life away… our lives away… that's on me," I confessed.

She shook her head. "We both thought Masterson would screw up. And he still might. But I don't want to keep punishing us for doing what we thought was best."

"Okay." I swallowed. "So… where do we go from here?"

"We work this out between us. Get back on track. Then we get married and have kids and live happily ever after with Billy, Jake, and Horace," she said.

"Okay," I repeated, my stomach unknotting. "I don't suppose we're ever going to see Hank and Mom again. Or our brother."

She shrugged. "They went into WITSEC voluntarily. They didn't want to be with us. So I guess they just don't get to be part of our family anymore."

"Their loss," I said.

"I think so, too." She put a hand on my chest. "Maybe we can start with a kiss?"

I laughed, feeling like I might cry tears of relief myself. But I held them back. "Jacey. When did we ever stop at just a kiss?"

She walked into my arms, and I wrapped my arms around her. "I love you, and I'm sorry," she said.

"I love you," I replied. "And I'm sorry, too."

Jacey leaned up, and our lips finally met after a month of torture. Everything slid back into place. I was home.

I licked her lips, and she let me in. Our tongues tangled gently then with more fervor.

She slid her hands up my chest, and only then did I remember how filthy I was. I captured her hands and kissed her fingertips. "I'm really grimy, baby. Maybe I should shower—"

"Okay," she said, her tone husky with deep kisses. "Let's shower."

Her words and her tone went straight to my groin. "We won't just be showering," I pointed out. "It's been a month. You sure you want our first time to be in the shower? Not that I'm complaining."

Jacey plastered herself against my body, and my breathing hitched. "I don't care where we do it. I just want to be with you. Now."

"Works for me," I smiled. I lifted her up, and she wrapped her legs around my waist and her arms around my neck. I looked for Billy as we stepped out the door, but he'd wisely made himself scarce. I quickly carried Jacey into the bathroom and shut the door behind us.

As I let her go, she slipped down my body, every inch of hers rubbing against every inch of mine. I had to squeeze my eyes closed and think of very non-sexy things to keep myself from getting too excited. I didn't want this to be over too soon.

She didn't seem to be of the same mind. Jacey began nibbling along my collarbone, her hand slipping down into my pants.

I groaned and caught her wrist. "Baby, I'm filthy. Let's get in the shower first."

With a sigh, she stopped and whipped her shirt over her head instead. My eyes zeroed in on her bra, and then that was gone as well. I licked my lips. Why had I insisted on the shower first again?

Oh yeah. My mind's not the only dirty thing here, I reminded myself. I stepped toward the shower-tub, and she moved with me, making it so that I had to press myself against those beautiful breasts in order to start the shower.

"You don't play fair," I complained.

In response, she unzipped my pants. "It's only playing if you don't intend to make good."

This time, I let her scoop my cock out. My pants and boxers fell to the floor while she stroked my shaft. Precum leaked freely from my dick. I was more than ready for her. I'd been more than ready for weeks.

Shower. SHOWER!!! I stopped her jerking me off and helped her into the tub then followed her in and closed the floral curtain.

Jacey went immediately for the soap, lathering up her hands and then starting to scrub me.

"You're trying to kill me, aren't you," I groaned when she washed my rigid cock.

"You said we couldn't do it until you were clean. I'm just being thorough," she teased.

I cupped her jaw and brought her in for a kiss then reached behind her to grab some soap myself. I started with 'thoroughly' soaping up her breasts.

She moaned, and her head dropped back, her long black hair cascading down to her ass. "Caleb…"

"Are you sure I'm clean?" I asked, which led to her getting more soap then me getting more soap.

Finally, the two of us couldn't stand it any longer. "Jacey..." I groaned at the same time she begged, "Caleb!"

I pressed her back against the tile. Her wet hair and body made it easy for me to lift her up against the tile and settle her down on my cock.

"Mfph," she grunted, and I realized, after a month, a little rubbing and scrubbing probably wasn't enough foreplay.

With an apologetic wince, I started to pull out. "Sorry, sorry. Too fast—"

"Caleb Killeen, if you pull out now, I will strangle you!" she bit out, clasping me to her and wrapping her legs around my waist to keep me from getting away.

I blinked, then chuckled. "Yes, ma'am." I fully sheathed myself in her again then just held her, letting her body adjust to mine once more.

It didn't take long. She rubbed impatiently against me just as I was going to start moving again. "Caleb, please!"

I gripped her hips and began thrusting, slow and steady. She clung to me and spurred me on with her heels.

"More!" she cried.

"As my lady commands," I said and went a bit harder and faster. She was so wet. So tight. I could have died right there of pleasure.

Still, I didn't cum until she did. When her inner muscles clamped around my cock, I had the most mind-blowing orgasm I'd ever experienced.

Jacey shook in my arms, and I knew she was equally affected. "Oh my God, Caleb," she moaned. "Oh my God."

I kissed her passionately. "That was nice, but let's not wait so long in between again, okay?"

"Okay," she agreed, still trembling against and around me.

I nuzzled her neck. "And next time you go into the city, I want to go with you."

She blushed. "Well, it was kind of a personal thing."

"Oh?" I asked. "Personal? What's so personal you don't want me there?"

"I went to the gynecologist," she giggled. "I'm not sure you'd have wanted to be there for that."

"I don't know about that. I am a big fan of your lady parts," I grinned. Then I sobered. "Is everything okay?"

Jacey chewed her lip. "Well... um... I... er... I got my Mirena taken out."

I blinked. "You did what?"

"I'm sorry. I should probably have said something before we had sex," she said in a rush. "But you looked so yummy... I kind of forgot..."

I let out a deep sigh. "Well, that's it then."

"That's what?" Jacey asked anxiously.

"I'm just going to have to marry you," I replied with a smile.

She swatted me. "Don't go scaring me like that!"

"Sorry," I said unapologetically. "So, what do you think?"

"I think it's a great idea," she responded with enthusiasm.

I nodded. "Good. I hope you feel the same way when I propose properly."

"There's nothing wrong with proposing just like this," she assured me. "In fact, I kind of like it."

"Still doing the one knee, ring, nice dinner thing. Or maybe a surprise," I mused aloud, thinking of the different ways I could propose.

Jacey cupped my cheek and kissed me. "I think this is perfect."

"Really?" I asked.

"Really," she said. "Now, we just need to ask Billy, Jake, and Horace to book us a church. No offense, but I've had about all I can take of judges."

"I agree." I smoothed a lock of hair off her face. "I love you, Jacey."

"I love you, Caleb," she echoed.

We kissed.

And then, we made love again.

EPILOGUE: LIVE AND LET GO

-Jacey-

"Mom? Where did Uncle Billy put the Fruity Pebbles?" McKenzie asked.

She'd been home from her first year of college a week and had already settled right in like she owned the place. Billy had taken to hiding the Fruity Pebbles they both liked, one, because he thought it was hilarious, and two, because he actually wanted the opportunity to have some. Our little snarfer had a tendency to eat the whole box before he even had a chance to sniff it.

Well, our not-so-little girl. I smiled at our nineteen-year-old summer baby. "I'd check the barn if I were you."

"Ew. Dad's in there feeding the cows. I don't think he has his shirt on." McKenzie wrinkled her nose.

I perked up. "Re-eally?"

"Oh my God, Mom, ewwww!" she made a gagging gesture.

"Come on, now. Don't tell me you haven't been eyeing some of those college hotties," I teased her.

"Well, yeah. But it's definitely not the same." She went through the cupboards a second time then dumped out the potato pot. "Aha! Score!"

I laughed. "I think I will go see your dad. Oh, don't forget, Uncle Jake and Uncle Horace are coming for dinner. We need to make extra, so don't go nibbling at the labeled food."

McKenzie gave me a mock-offended look. "When would I ever?"

"Says last summer's fruit salad," Caleb said, wiping his face on a cloth while he walked into the house.

"Oh my God, put a shirt on!" she complained, shielding her eyes. She got out a mixing bowl and started dumping Fruity Pebbles inside.

"Which of our cows do you need me to go grab in order to accommodate that amount of cereal?" her father chuckled.

She stuck her head in the fridge again. "Nah, no need. There's enough here."

"That's code for: Dad, we're going to need more milk if we're going to cook anything for supper," I said.

"I heard it loud and clear." My husband walked over and dropped a kiss on top of my head while he toweled off his chest. He'd retained a very nice body. But then, we were young parents.

McKenzie flopped down on the sofa with her mixing bowl of Fruity Pebbles, leaving the empty box on the counter for Billy to find. "I'm bored. Not a lot happens around here, you know? I mean, I don't think anyone in town has ever even stolen a car. It's so quiet. College is a lot more exciting."

"Trust me. A boring life is a nice life," I said, smiling up at Caleb.

"Pfft. How would you know? You've been here all your lives. I mean, it was nice of Uncle Billy to raise you and all, and it's great Dad's a vet, but it's soooo boring," she sighed.

"We could watch the game," her father suggested.

McKenzie rolled her eyes. "It's only fun when you watch it live in the stadium, and college baseball is better anyway."

"Our little McKenzie, such a sports snob," I said.

"Yeah, well, someone has to be. The highlight of your lives is watching *Wheel of Fortune* with Uncle Billy," she scoffed, munching on her cereal.

"Yep, that's all the excitement we've ever had," Caleb agreed.

I nodded. It was best she never knew what had happened before she was born. I didn't want her living in fear.

And we had no reason to anymore, as far as I could tell. As far as we knew, Masterson was in prison for another five years. The sheik was still on the run. All ransoms on our heads had been canceled, or, if they hadn't, no one had managed to find us.

It had been a difficult, hair-raising decision, but we finally decided to allow McKenzie to go to the U of M. Not that we could have stopped her, but I'd been biting my nails the whole year, hoping McKenzie Kent wouldn't be singled out by danger.

We were Kents now, which was fine by me. I knew in my heart I was a Killeen. Anything to keep us safe.

"Have you met any boys?" I asked, winking at Caleb.

"Please. Freshman boys are still *so* immature. Dad's like five years older than you, right? That's probably about how many years I'm going to need between me and my husband." Her tone carried such authority that I had to stifle a smile.

"Of course," her father said. "Men just don't mature as fast. You should go pick a ripe, old, wrinkly one."

"Dad!!!" she protested. "Ugh, you two, I swear!"

There was a knock at the door.

Caleb glanced that way with a frown. "Who could it be at this hour? It's too soon for Jake or Horace to be here."

"Maybe it's someone campaigning for the election again," I said.

McKenzie rolled her eyes. "I hate those people. It's not like I don't already know who I'm voting for. I'll be in my room." She took the bowl and headed upstairs while her father went to the door.

The man beyond it looked to be in his thirties. He wore a tailored suit and loafers. A Rolex watch rested on his wrist, and he had diamond cufflinks. The whole ensemble might have cost more than the farm.

"Mr. Killeen?" he asked, straightening his jacket.

"Oh God," I whispered, horror washing over me. "He's found us."

BONUS CHAPTER: THE ABSOLUTE TRUTH

-Will-

I sat behind my grandfather's desk, bored again. After private schools, Yale, and Harvard Business School, I was bored out of my mind. I'd followed my expected trajectory. I'd done everything expected of me.

Only once did I ever step a toe out of line. Well, almost. I suggested, at one of my visits to his cushy prison, that I might like to play football seriously. Not just as an extracurricular for my transcripts, but as a real, devout player.

William Masterson Sr. had blown a gasket. I was grounded, deprived of my electronics, and carted off to a very strict boarding school for the summer, forcing me to not participate in football at all. He'd very reluctantly let me play again until I finished college, but only with the understanding I was being groomed to take over the family business.

The problem was, some guy named Ike Freeborn handled most of the business. I was mostly window dressing, shaking hands, attending galas and charity events. When I asked for more responsibility, Ike looked at me like I'd lost my mind.

I rocked back in the big, intimidating, wingback chair. Ike would even ask me to leave the office sometimes to do business deals. He was actually intimidating. I was…

… like little Simba in the *Lion King*? Except I was getting the impression I was *never* going to be ascending the throne.

Speaking of Ike, there was a knock on the office door.

"Come in," I sighed.

Ike wandered in with two men in business suits behind him. All I saw all day long were men in business suits coming into the office while I walked out. "Sir," he said, and it always sounded as though it pained him to say it, "I was hoping we could use your office for a quick meeting."

'Quick meeting' meant at least an hour. I nodded and stood. "Go right ahead. I was just going to go check on the Jasper File."

The 'Jasper File' was code for 'I'm going to go do fucking nothing, but I need to sound important in front of the clients.' Though I was pretty sure the clients didn't care. They rarely ever even looked at me.

I walked out, and they walked in, Ike closing the door firmly behind them. They were thick doors, impossible to listen through. I knew because I'd tried.

Dawn was sitting at her desk, as usual, headphones on, fielding calls and doing whatever she did with the files. She was supposedly my assistant, but mostly she was Ike's. A very nice girl named Heather took care of my travel arrangements and various public engagements and interviews.

"Mr. Masterson," Dawn said deferentially.

"Hi Dawn," I replied. "How's the little mite?"

She patted her very round belly. "Any minute now, he'll come make an appearance."

"You make sure you take the full maternity leave, okay? I don't care what Ike says," I told her.

Dawn smiled at me and shook her head. "Mr. Freeborn needs me. I'll just be three weeks and then—" Her face suddenly went green. "Oh dear. Excuse me, Mr. Masterson!" She ran from her desk toward the bathrooms.

I shook my head. Poor Dawn had experienced a truly awful pregnancy.

… At the docks at midnight. And if one of them screams, you just shoot her. Then the other women will just fall into line. It sounded like Ike.

What the fuck?! I realized Dawn had left her headset on. Likely, she'd been taking notes for Ike. I sat down, wondering what the hell I was hearing, and put the headphones on myself.

"… Need to get them to the brothel as quickly as possible. The cops have been sniffing around, and not the ones we can bribe, either," another voice said. This one was definitely not Ike.

Brothel? I frowned in confusion.

"We'll send a clean-up crew if we need to," Ike responded in an offhand manner. "There's more of those where they came from."

If I wasn't crazy and hallucinating this, Ike was talking to these two bastards about human trafficking!

Oh, Ike was in so much shit once my grandfather found out.

I dropped the headphones and was about to go striding into the office to break up their nefarious little clique when I looked at Dawn's screen. She'd left it unlocked.

There was a folder open I'd never seen on the server before.

I glanced over the monitor to make sure Dawn wasn't on her way back then began clicking through files. With every file, my stomach dropped further and further.

This wasn't Ike's doing. I could see my grandfather's signature on many documents pertaining to everything from drugs, to weapons, to human trafficking.

My stomach roiled. Dawn wasn't the only one who was going to be sick. But I swallowed the bile in my throat. I didn't want to lose this opportunity to see what the company was really doing.

I quickly copied the hidden folder and uploaded it to myself on my personal Google Drive. By the time Dawn returned, still dabbing her mouth, I was leaning casually against her desk, pretending for all the world that I hadn't done a damn thing.

"Feeling any better?" I asked with my best, convincing Masterson smile.

"A bit." She sat down and picked up her headphones. "This pregnancy has been the worst."

"It seems like it," I said sympathetically. "Well, I'm going to go see if we're missing anything in the supply closet. Might as well make myself useful somehow."

Dawn nodded and went back to her listening and note taking.

I had to keep myself from running as I made my way to an empty office. I closed and locked the door behind me, then took out my phone and brought up the file. I spent the next hour familiarizing myself with what appeared to be the real family business. Or businesses, as it were.

My grandfather was not at all what he seemed to be, and insider trading was the very least of his crimes.

Now that I had all this information, what the hell was I supposed to do with it? Go to the authorities? Confront my grandfather? Both?

First, I thought I'd better confront Ike because he'd been doing all this on my grandfather's behalf right under my nose.

I was steeling myself to do just that when I stumbled upon a subfolder labeled simply 'The Trial.'

Curious, I opened it. Inside, I found depositions and court transcripts. I skimmed them, finding that the authorities already knew about my grandfather and that he hadn't gone to prison for insider trading at all.

So, he was being punished for crimes he was continuing? That didn't seem right. One would think you'd be unable to commit crimes from prison. But, apparently, I was wrong.

Continuing down the rabbit hole, I found another folder labeled 'The Killeens.'

I remembered Jocelyn and Caleb had appeared prominently in the trial transcripts, testifying against my grandfather as the final nail in his coffin. Caleb's last name was 'Killeen.'

After I opened the folder, I immediately wished I hadn't. There were videos inside of a young couple... coupling... in the mansion I called home. It didn't appear as though they knew they were being watched and recorded. Other videos showed... my father with them.

Not en flagrant, no. But sharing moments of friendship, also carefully cataloged in this multitude of videos.

My sense of dignity wouldn't allow me to peruse the videos too much, however. I felt dirty watching the Killeens.

More documents detailed correspondence between my grandfather and some sheik, plotting to kill them both.

But, most damning of all, was a folder labeled 'Surrogate.'

Inside, I learned Mrs. Killeen had carried me herself after my grandfather arranged for invitro fertilization with a donor egg and my biological father's sperm. From what I could tell from the videos in that file, she'd basically been drugged and held prisoner.

I wasn't sure if I was more disgusted by these personal violations or the bad my grandfather did out in the wider world. Either way, I couldn't stomach any of it. I'd heard of evil, of course, but I never thought I'd be raised to perpetrate it.

"So, I think you've been doing some snooping," Ike said, leaning in the doorway.

My eyes snapped upward, and I was sure I wasn't hiding the hatred in them very well. "What the hell is all this?"

"Your inheritance. You know, this makes it easier. Your grandfather and I were trying to figure out how to bring you onboard, but now you've been properly informed. You will, of course, attend the meetings from now on..." Ike informed me.

"Not on your life," I growled. "I don't want anything to do with this shit."

Ike rolled his eyes. "Your grandfather was afraid you'd turned out weak. Like your father."

"Don't you talk about my father!" I yelled.

He came into the office and closed the door behind him. "Do you want the whole office to hear you?"

"Maybe. Maybe I want the whole world to hear. He's been doing these things from prison! Jesus!" I turned my phone to face him and played one of the repulsive sex videos. "What the fuck am I supposed to do with *this?!*"

Ike sat down across from me. "Will, have you ever heard the

phrase, 'To make an omelet, you have to break a few eggs'? This is the cost of the life of luxury you enjoy. These people betrayed your grandfather. They took advantage of his good nature. They—"

"They were fucking kids, they were fucking desperate, and *he* took advantage of *them*. Don't you try to fucking twist things on me!" I shouted. "Don't you *dare*."

He sighed and stood. "Your drive will be scrubbed, and you will be placed under house arrest. There were contingencies made for this, of course. Hopefully, you won't do something stupid and kill yourself like your father did. Then we'd have to start the whole process over again."

"Process? What, you're going to tie down another young girl and force her to give birth to a brother of mine?!" I asked, horrified.

"Probably a son. But yes, if we have to. Now, I've already called security…" he said.

I scowled at him. "I suppose you think I'm just going tra-la, tra-lee along with security just like that, huh?"

"That's the idea, yes," he smirked.

"Hmm. I'm going to have to say 'no' to that request," I replied.

"And what exactly do you think you're going to do about it?" he snorted.

The door opened behind him, and there stood two security guards.

"Did you know I played football in college?" I asked.

Ike's eyebrows drew together in confusion. "Yes. I am aware."

I kicked the desk at him with all my strength. He topped over in his chair with a loud 'oomph.'

Then security was on me, but I tackled one against the wall. He hit his head and slid down.

The second was just starting to call for back-up, trying to stop me with an arm around my throat, but that was his mistake. I slammed my elbows back into his ribs then stamped my foot down on the phone he dropped.

"Fuck, man!" the guard groaned, holding his ribs and sinking to his knees.

I didn't stay to see if any of the three men were all right. I dashed out of the office and to the stairs. I wasn't getting stuck in there.

There were several floors, but I was in good shape. I bolted all the way to the bottom. I burst out of the building and into sharp daylight.

I'd never been so happy to see the sun. I looked around, then, for the first time in my life, ran across the street and jumped onto a city bus.

I slapped my credit card on the reader, and, only when the bus was underway, did I sit down.

"Rough day?" the driver asked.

"The worst," I said.

"Well, don't worry about it. It's bound to get better," he replied with an encouraging smile.

I managed a smile back, that may have been more of a grimace. *Bound to get better?*

I doubted it.

Book 5 coming soon!

ALSO BY M. FRANCIS HASTINGS

Once Bitten

Submitting to My Stepbrother series

Stranded With My Stepbrother

Snatched With My Stepbrother

Sequestered With My Stepbrother

Subpoenaed With My Stepbrother

The Beguiling Baronets series

Deceiving the Duke

Dream Mates

Dream Weaver

Dream Reader

Sign up for my newsletter here: https://subscribepage.io/TfsA3A